CROSSED OVER

A COMING OUT STORY

SANTANA KNOX

Editor: Alexa, The Fiction Fix

ev Editor: R.N Barbosa

ver/Interior art: B. B., @FlashFryed

CROSSED OVER PLAYLIST
AVAILABLE ON SPOTIFY

You wouldn't like me - Tegan and Sara
Shark Smile - Edit - Big Thief
Pisces - Rebecka Reinhard
Meet Me At Our Spot - The Anxiety, willow
Wake up Exhausted - Tegan and Sara
Margaret (feat. Bleachers) - Lana Del Rey
Silk Chiffon - MUNA, Phoebe Bridgers
Vampire Empire - Big Thief
This is Everything - Tegan and Sara
Kick Drum Heart - The Avett Brothers
Mr. Brightside - Hayley Kiyoko
I've Got Friends - Manchester Orchestra
I Won't Be Left - Tegan and Sara
To a Poet - First Aid Kit
Fell in Love With a Girl - The White Stripes
HOT TO GO! - Chappell Roan
Will You Return - The Avett Brothers
Pretty Girls Make Graves - The Smiths
You Have Been Loved - Sia

DERBY LINGO:

Blocker - The positional Skaters who form the Pack. Up to four Blockers from each team may skate per Jam. One Blocker per Jam, for each team, may be a Pivot Blocker.

Bout - a roller derby "game" with two, thirty-minute halves.

Fresh meat - a skater who hasn't passed their minimum requirements test and is not eligible to bout.

Gear - roller derby equipment: skates, protective wear, mouthguards, helmet.

Hockey stop - An abrupt stop using the sides of the skates.

Jam - a basic unit of time during a bout, a jam lasts two minutes.

Jammer - the point scorer for the team, only one on the track per team.

Panty - a slip cover for the helmet to designate the jammer and the pivot.

Pivot - a Blocker with extra abilities and responsibilities.

Quads - roller derby skates (two wheels in the front, two in the back).

Rink rash - a burn caused from bare skin rubbing against the waxed floor.

Scrimmage - a practice/friendly bout between teammates.

Snow plowing - a beginner stop where the knees move in and out until the skates roll to a slow stop.

Taking a knee – happens when injuries occur.

Turn stop/derby stop - stopping technique where skater turns around and stops abruptly on their toe stops.

The star - the helmet cover (panty) for Jammers containing two stars, one on each side.

The stripe- the pivot helmet cover (panty) with a stripe down the middle.

WFTDA - Women's Flat Track Derby Association.

Zebra – referee.

FLAT TRACK ROLLER DERBY GUIDE

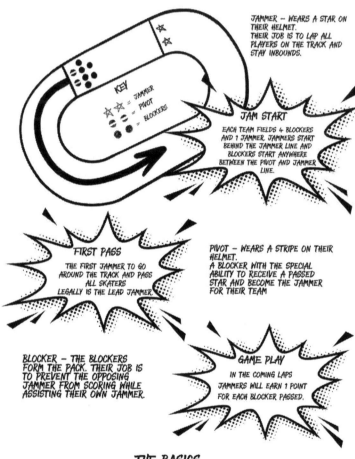

JAMMER — WEARS A STAR ON THEIR HELMET.
THEIR JOB IS TO LAP ALL PLAYERS ON THE TRACK AND STAY INBOUNDS.

KEY
✩ ✩ = JAMMER
⊘ ⊘ = PIVOT
● ● = BLOCKERS

JAM START

EACH TEAM FIELDS 4 BLOCKERS AND 1 JAMMER. JAMMERS START BEHIND THE JAMMER LINE AND BLOCKERS START ANYWHERE BETWEEN THE PIVOT AND JAMMER LINE.

FIRST PASS

THE FIRST JAMMER TO GO AROUND THE TRACK AND PASS ALL SKATERS LEGALLY IS THE LEAD JAMMER.

PIVOT — WEARS A STRIPE ON THEIR HELMET.
A BLOCKER WITH THE SPECIAL ABILITY TO RECEIVE A PASSED STAR AND BECOME THE JAMMER FOR THEIR TEAM

BLOCKER — THE BLOCKERS FORM THE PACK. THEIR JOB IS TO PREVENT THE OPPOSING JAMMER FROM SCORING WHILE ASSISTING THEIR OWN JAMMER.

GAME PLAY

IN THE COMING LAPS JAMMERS WILL EARN 1 POINT FOR EACH BLOCKER PASSED.

THE BASICS

*BOUT — A ROLLER DERBY GAME
*TWO TEAMS MATCH AGAINST EACH OTHER IN A BOUT
*A BOUT CONTAINS TWO THIRTY MINUTE PERIODS
*EACH PERIOD CONTAINS MULTIPLE "JAMS"
*A JAM CAN LAST UP TO TWO MINUTES
*LEGAL CONTACT — HIPS, REAR AND SHOULDERS
*ILLEGAL CONTACT/BLOCK AREAS — BACK, TRIPPING, ELBOWING

Explicit language, on page sexual activity, poverty trauma, first-generation trauma, injury trauma, conflict between mother and daughter, emesis, inappropriate/unethical therapist-patient relationship, car accident, head injury, stitches without anesthesia, PTSD, marijuana use, alcoholism recovery, denial of sexual identity, death.

It's never too late

The announcer's overly alert voice came through the speakers. *"Nia-Death Experience* passes *Tonna Hips,* but *Reese Ender* checks and—oh! That's a stumble, but she recovers, nearly tripping over the still-fallen *Britney Fears.* Can we get a medic on the track?"

He was distracting as hell, and I was feeling that last slam. Reese Ender was a heavy hitter, and I knew I'd be black and blue before the morning. Worst of all, it was extra hot on the track tonight with all the lights set up for the film crew. They were televising this for some streaming special on TvFlix, and our rink parent, Lonnie, was seeing dollar signs at the prospect of fame, enthralled with the idea of people coming to Devil Town to watch us play and spend their hard earned money at Skateland.

Sweat dripped down my chest, and my fishnets itched under my shorts at the thought of everyone I knew watching, but I pumped my thighs with every ounce of energy I still had left. I moved with a desperate force, one foot in front of the other, crossing over as I circled the track, fifteen feet away from stealing the win from the *Wolverine Dreams* Roller Derby team.

I'd been killing myself all season, promising our team we'd finally dethrone these bitches. It was our turn, and winning the state championship would give us first pick access of Skateland for our practices. Lonnie loved us, but they needed the rent money from other teams in nearby towns using the track. They couldn't turn that down.

This win would give us the advantage we needed to stay winners; it was the very reason the Wolverines had been reigning supreme for four years in a row.

I was two seconds away from changing that.

My heart pounded in my throat. As a jammer, everything came down to me. I was the entire point system. I *was* the ball, and the finish line was my goal, as long as Reese Ender stayed behind me.

"*Nia! Nia! Nia!*" The crowd shouted to my right as I circled the track.

I lifted my fingers in the air, raising them to my head for a two-finger salute—a little show of cockiness—before I crossed the jammer line.

My brain rattled inside my head before I'd even noticed my skates weren't on the ground anymore. My teeth clanked painfully inside my mouth, my tongue splitting from the blunt force of my canines tearing flesh as liquid iron pooled around my gums. Simultaneously, my back hit the floor, a sick crunch beneath me raging through my body in an agonizing wave of pain.

"Oh sh—" The announcer's microphone was still on.

"Take a knee!" Lonnie's voice boomed through the crowd, and it went silent around me.

"Call an ambulance," I heard not far off in the distance.

I blinked my eyes open to see Reese Ender standing above me, a ghost-white expression painted over her face.

"Her leg," she said, a retching sound coming from another direction just as my eyes flickered closed once more.

I had to be suffering from dumb-bitch syndrome.

There was no reason for me to do this. How the hell she convinced me to go through with it was beyond me. Sure, there was always the constant nagging that I couldn't let my fear rule me, but the exercise itself felt ridiculous.

I didn't need to prove anything to myself.

I was perfectly fine not being the same girl I once was.

No gym bag in my hand, no plans to stay long enough to get sweaty or change, I walked through the double doors, two fingers hooked around the laces of my quad roller skates.

"This is a closed practice," the person behind the glass booth says, not bothering to look up at me from counting the money in the drawer.

Dark rimmed glasses sat on top of a narrow nose, and a long brown ponytail plumed from the top of their head.

"Lonnie said I could come skate whenever..." I murmured, my shoulders sagging with defeat.

"Oh shit, well, if you know Lonnie, it's fine. Just try to stay out of the skaters' way. The Devil's Dames are practicing." They tilted their head to the skaters running drills and ladders.

I sighed, my hopes for the rink being empty vanishing into thin air.

I should have known better. Lonnie's rink was the only one in the tri-state area. There were probably at least four teams battling at all times to use this place for their practices and bouts.

"I know that sigh. You one of us?" They stood, a newspaper in hand as they walked out of the booth, tilting their chin up at me like they were waiting for an answer.

"Once upon a time. Practically a lifetime ago, though." I looked down at my quads, the laces all messed up and tangled, my wheels the ones I used outside on the pavement the last time I even wore these things. If I put them on these freshly waxed floors, they'd likely scuff them up to hell.

To top it off, I hadn't skated in five years.

Cruz Credo, Antônia. That's what my mother would say.

What the hell was I doing out here? During a practice? I was gonna embarrass myself in front of skaters who were *actually* capable of staying on a roller derby team.

"They could use a Jammer. I assume you weren't a blocker." They laughed, an obvious jab at my small frame.

"I don't play anymore." I shook my head. "Maybe I'll just go, come back when the rink is open to the public."

"Of course she doesn't skate anymore. Look at her, Mo," said a voice behind me.

I clicked my tongue. I really didn't think I'd get recognized.

"You're not Nia-Death?" She tilted her head like a curious dog.

I tensed.

"No way! I heard they had to completely rebuild your leg," Mo said, more excited about the brutality of the injury than anything else.

My cheeks flushed with heat, my palms sweating, and me, hating the way they were both looking at me.

Was it possible to exist without existing to other people?

"I guess she probably doesn't wanna get hurt again." The helmeted girl crossed her arms, antagonizing me.

"I'm not dumb. You think I don't know the lengths a desperate derby team would go to in order to fill a jammer position?" I raised a single eyebrow. "Including insulting a total stranger as a way to bait them into practicing with you? As if I have some sort of insane over-competitive need to prove you wrong? Because I don't. If you know who I am, you know I have no semblance of an ego left." I scoffed.

"That's too bad, princess. Would have been fun to see how fast you can get to twenty-seven laps around the ring. You know... *fill* that *jammer* position." She smirked, brushing wisps of blonde hair away from her face before walking away.

"Get in the pack, Harvey!" Mo commanded, slapping her arm with the now rolled-up newspaper.

I laughed louder than I intended to, and a few heads turned our way from lacing up their skates. I clamped my mouth shut.

"I'll leave before I'm any more of a distraction. Thank

you, Mo." I waved them off, walking out the doors and going back to my car.

I was twenty-two when I ran away, tail tucked between my broken legs. It took months of grueling physical therapy to learn to walk again, to trust my body once more. Now, five years later, here I was, back in the very place that forgot me.

I sat for a moment, the heat turned on, snowflakes melting on my windshield while the fog built up on the windows. I looked up, seeing the same blonde girl from before looking through the rink's glass entrance.

It would be crazy.

Absolutely insane.

I didn't have insurance; if I got hurt this time, I'd literally just have to put ice on it and hope it was good enough. My knee throbbed at the memory of sliding on my ass through the rink with my leg bent sideways, my shin bone sticking out of my flesh, a dull ache that never tempered.

I grimaced.

Fucking PTSD.

That was what my shrink called it, anyway, when I tried to explain to her I couldn't close my eyes without seeing it happening on repeat, couldn't purge the image of my mangled legs in the dark of my mind.

Five years.

One session every week.

That was how long it took for her to convince me the only way to get over it was to get back on the figurative horse.

My skates.

I dialed her number.

"You're spiraling again, Antônia," she said, far too calm and collected for how chaotic I felt internally.

"No, there's just...I'll do it tomorrow. The rink is full," I rushed to say.

"Full?" she questioned me with suspicion.

"There's a derby practice going on right now," I said awkwardly, hoping she wouldn't make too big of a deal about it.

"Don't you think that's the perfect opportunity?" I knew she would fucking do that.

She always jumped at the chance for me to expose my fears and traumas in the most dramatic way. I couldn't just be eased into something. She wanted me to dive in headfirst.

"Would you be saying this to any of your other patients right now? Under the same conditions?" I asked.

"You're not any patient." She cleared her throat.

"Obviously. Tomorrow. I promise, okay?" I lied.

"Keep me updated. Beijo." She blew a kiss over the phone.

"Beijo, tchau." I hung up, my heavy exhale creating more fog inside the car.

That was the thing about my mother—she was the smartest person I knew, capable of all sorts of rationale, fully examining a situation from every angle before speaking on it. She knew exactly why anyone's behavior presented in a certain way.

It's what made her fantastic at her job.

But when it came to me, all rationale dissolved. The fault was always in myself and in the person I chose to become, despite all her attempts to right the course.

If my cousins were rebelling, they had every right. She could pull any reason from her book and say they were justified. *Pobrezinhos.* If I rebelled? I was a spoiled little brat with no gratitude for anything I'd been given.

If I couldn't break from a depressive episode? I wasn't trying hard enough. I was weak, allowing myself to succumb to it. If her best friend had the sads? *Que tragedia.* She would drop everything to go tend to the woman on her hands and knees.

My pain was never valid enough to her.

Until it became physical. When the injury happened, there was finally a form of pain, of failure she could acknowledge without admitting her own defeat, without it being linked back as her own negligence.

For me, it was an opportunity for self-reflection. The way I had been treating my body, I had been going so hard, it was practically a form of self-harm. Punishment. The all or nothing mentality had finally caught up to me, and I could no longer ignore it knocking on my door.

No. Knocking *down* my door.

The change in my behavior with the hard-proof of x-rays gave my mother something tangible to hold onto. It was a weakness in me she could acknowledge existed because of *me.* It didn't somehow reflect back onto her, not the way my other failures did.

I put the key in the ignition and started the car.

The girl was no longer at the window, and the adrenaline rush of *almost* doing the thing had worn off. The only remaining evidence, the sweat still lingering on my palms.

Tomorrow, I could try again.

Maybe.

I drove away from the rink, heading in the direction of the kitchenette I'd rented when I came into town the day before. This was a one stop mission: drop into the hellhole that was Devil Town, skate some trauma away, then move on.

And by moving on, I'd be driving straight through to New York for the job waiting for me. Small town life wasn't calling to me anymore. Everyone knew me here, once upon a time, and I just wanted to be somewhere that I wasn't recognized. My mother wouldn't let me move on if I was still carrying the emotional scars of my injury.

She called it a clean slate, a place for me to start over where no one knew me.

Sure, college was a little like that, but I didn't go too far from Devil Town, and my story traveled far.

It's all in your head. No one cares that much. My mother's voice donned the overly professional tone she took anytime she made her personal opinions my problem to deal with. *It's just a silly little roller derby. You're not in the NFL.*

Sure, maybe no one cared. But then why was it all anyone could think to say to me?

Hey, you're the girl who jacked up her leg, right?

Hey everyone, this is Nia. She's basically a pro skater!

Nia, there're skates here. Why don't you show us some tricks?

It was never ending. It would always follow me unless I put serious distance between us.

The phone rang once more, and I didn't have to bet money on it to be sure it was my mom calling again, urging me to turn around and join the others in their practice.

She didn't even care about roller derby. The four years I

played, she never once showed up to a single bout. But people knew me in a positive light, and because of that, she was indifferent about it.

No one prepared me for the burden it was to be the singular child of an immigrant, the pressure to not just succeed, but surpass, my parents' accomplishments, as well as their struggles. To be better than they ever could be, since they sacrificed so much to make it so.

Anything less was a spit in their face.

A blemish over their efforts to provide me with a better life, a better chance.

Sure, my Bachelor's degree was fine, but my mother had multiple PhDs in neuroscience and psychology, and it would take years to match that kind of greatness in her eyes. I went to college? She studied harder. I was having a hard time? Her life had been harder. No one could make me hate myself like a ten-minute phone call with my mother could.

Yet, despite it all, she was still my best friend.

Hell, she was my freaking *therapist*.

Sure, I tried seeing others, tried figuring out for myself if there was a healthier way to heal than by the same person who caused my pain. Half the problem was my lack of money, and that she didn't charge me. The other half was the absence of Latin American health professionals, so anytime my mother would push me over the edge of reason, we'd break up, cut contact, and I'd scour the web for hours in search of a shrink who could possibly fathom the entirety of what it was to grow up under the shadow of an immigrant parent.

I could never find one I could afford, so I'd settle for whoever took my insurance and hoped they could do a fraction of what my mother could do for me without the added damage.

They never could. One or two sessions was the most I could tolerate. It wasn't their fault; how could I blame them for not understanding an identity-shaping experience?

"You have no idea how tiring it is to be your daughter," I answered in my snippiest tone.

"You have no idea how tiring it is to mother *and* doctor you, Tônia." She reminded me that it wasn't her who'd asked for this dynamic, but me.

Every time I dropped a therapist, I went crawling back, promising not to cross the boundaries of our professional relationship with my personal shit.

It never worked, but she tolerated me anyway.

I needed help.

We both knew that.

"I told you I'd try tomorrow. What do you need?" I said with a heavy exhale, trying to merge the call with my car so I could use both hands to drive.

"Respeito," she cut in, letting me know this was a *mom* call, not a *doctor* call. "I just wanted to check that you already sent the deposit for your apartment in SoHo."

Shit. I forgot.

"Yes, I did. I'm not completely useless," I lied, putting on a snide tone, more annoyed that she knew me better than I could tolerate.

"I'll be flying back in the week after; we can go furniture shopping for your new place together." She used the sickly-sweet voice she always wore when she was buying my affection.

She couldn't help it—this was how it'd always been with

her. Unfortunately for me, I was too broke to have any moral reservations about it. I'd take her money gladly; otherwise, I'd be sleeping on a cold floor in an unfurnished apartment until I'd gotten at least a couple paychecks to help stay afloat.

"I'd like that," I admitted with the foolish reservation of a girl who'd always crave salvaging the relationship we'd never truly have.

A loud honk pulled me out of the trance I didn't realize I was in, barely in time to swerve out of the way from an incoming semi-truck.

"Crap!" I yelled, taking my foot off the gas once I felt the ice under my tires steal the car from my control.

The bridge was too slippery, my chevy spinning once and then a second time before my brain told my body to cooperate.

The breaks.

My thigh mustered the shaky strength to lift my foot over the pedal and slam down on the third spin, my vision nearly black from adrenaline, my throat hoarse from screaming.

The side of my head smacked against the glass with a hard thump just as the airbag exploded into my face, sending me back into the headrest violently. My teeth were the last things to rattle, the sound of them clashing against each other more unnerving than the prolonged honk of my horn.

My head rang from the inside out, a pain reminiscent of a sharp ax, splitting my skull down the middle. The car alarm brayed, forcing my eyes open to find the tree had settled in nicely halfway through the hood.

"Antônia, are you driving? Antônia? I can't believe you'd be so reckless as to..." Her voice faded away as the ringing pierced deeper into my brain.

It was just like my mother to chastise me at a time like this.

Nausea swept through my body as the pain intensified. A sleepiness washed over me that even the relentless honk of my broken horn couldn't dissuade me from. I hung my chin down, the seatbelt still holding me in place as I shut my eyes once again.

"**S**hit. She looks hurt. Hey, Nia-Death." A voice pulled me out of the darkness.

I attempted to mumble, but even my brain couldn't decipher the garbled speech coming from my mouth.

"Harvey, should we call 911?" Another voice came from a distance.

"No!" I managed to blurt out, my heart racing at the thought of another ambulance bill forcing me back into crippling debt.

Once was enough.

My eyes shot open, the headache blinding me from the sheer pain hammering through my skull.

It was her, the girl from the rink.

There was someone else with her too, but I didn't recognize them.

"I'm okay," I mumbled, reaching for the clip of my scatbelt.

"Your head is bleeding. You should stay put until we get someone out here."

"If you call an ambulance, you're paying for it," I growled, pushing up from my seat and stumbling out of the car.

I immediately fell into her, caught just before I collapsed onto the ground.

"Let me guess—no hospital either?" she said in a snarky tone.

I shook my head, confirming it.

There was no judgment in the way she looked at me, just the exasperated sound of someone who wasn't sure how to help.

"I'll be okay. I'm staying at Lorraine's Inn. If you can take me there, I can call for a tow and deal with this shit in the morning." I rubbed my temple, feeling the gash past my hairline.

She cocked an eyebrow, like she wasn't sure I was in the best state to be making sound decisions.

"I gotta drop off Nadine over that direction anyway. Come on, let's get you in the car."

The friend she called Nadine positioned herself under my right arm while the blonde ducked under my left and they helped me to the backseat of her SUV.

"Do you have anything you need in there?" she asked.

"Crap," I groaned. "I have a few bags in the trunk."

I slouched down, laying across the backseat of her monstrosity of a vehicle, but before I could succumb to the beckoning of my heavy eyelids, the slam of the doors shutting around me brought me back.

"You doing okay? It's probably better if you don't sleep," She said nervously, turning the key in the ignition.

I mumbled out an "I'm so tired" as I fought against my eyes' heavy blinking.

Both girls looked at each other but remained silent.

"We're only twenty minutes out from the emergency room in Daysville. Are you sure I can't take you there?" Our eyes met through the reflection of the rearview mirror.

"No." I gritted out. "It's just a little cut. It'll stop bleeding soon. It just needs some super glue."

Her friend chuckled from the passenger seat.

"Let me at least call one of our teammates to come stitch you up. She's a nurse," She bartered.

I didn't answer.

I could only focus on the force of the pain drilling my head open.

"Hey." The blonde shook my shoulder.

"Yeah, yeah," I murmured, swatting her away.

When I opened my eyes again, the pounding in my head had subsided, and all I could feel was my dry mouth. I whimpered, wincing at the bright lights overhead while my brain attempted to piece together our location.

Too yellow to be hospital lighting, but then the glow of blonde hair absorbed all the light like an eclipse, blocking out the sun as she leaned over me, far too close for comfort.

"You're alive!" she said, a little too shocked.

"Where am I?" I groaned, trying to prop my elbows up

on what I could now see was a brown leather couch, my head still spinning.

I grabbed the edges of the cushions, squeezing tightly as I held on for dear life while the room whirled by in a vicious fury.

Vicious Fury, great derby name.

I still did that. Even though it had been years since I skated, I ached to make the connection wherever I could.

So why did I chicken out at the rink?

Because scarier than failing was succeeding.

What in the world was supposed to happen if I went in there? If I skated the twenty-seven in five and conquered all my demons? If I managed to go through a session without falling and breaking all my bones again?

Not knowing was easier.

Safer.

"Don't sit up too quickly; you banged your head pretty hard on the steering wheel. Or maybe it was the window?" The blonde brought her thumb to her lip, as if it somehow helped her think.

"Where am I?" I asked again, this time not bothering to lift myself up.

From what I could see, it was an apartment. Nothing crazy or out of the ordinary: early 2000s remodel of what was likely a far older building.

"My place," another voice called. I followed it to find a redhead with a pixie cut sitting on a kitchen counter with a mug to her lips. "I'm Nadine." She half-waved.

She was no longer in practice clothes, her hair slightly wet, as if, in the time it'd taken me to regain consciousness, she had already showered and changed.

"You looked rough, and you kept refusing the hospital." Brushing wisps of hair from her eyes and tucking it behind overly pierced ears, the blonde turned to the coffee table before passing a glass of water my way. "Do you need help sitting up?" She raised a questioning eyebrow. "I'm Harvey."

"I can manage," I rasped, my voice hoarse and my throat too scratchy. "Not my first accident," I joked, lifting myself too fast and blinking hard at the oncoming dizzy spell. I pushed down the rush of nausea threatening at the base of my jaw.

"I'm Antônia. Nia, if you want." I winced through the introduction, a throbbing pulse manifesting at my temple.

"Woah there, not too fast," Nadine cautioned.

"Look, I'm grateful, but I don't want to inconvenience anyone." I reached for my things on the coffee table, but tattooed hands were quicker to snatch my keys before I could grab them.

"I don't know where you think you're going, but you have a concussion." The one named Harvey shook her head, tossing my car keys into the pockets of her cargo pants. "You'll stay here until Mercy can check you out and clear you." She casually sauntered to the door.

My "who?" came out almost mechanically.

"She's our resident nurse," Nadine chirped, setting her mug down and hopping off the counter. "She's already on her way, and if you say no, Harvey will just take you to the emergency room instead."

Crap.

How awkward.

I tried my best to avoid contact with these very people,

and now, I was going to be forced to interact with them. Harvey revealed a mischievous half-smirk as she turned the doorknob, and with a tilt of her head alone, she commanded Nadine in her direction.

"Wait, where are you going?" I asked, suddenly confused as to why the room was clearing out when I was the stranger here.

"I work some odd shifts at the grocery store," the redhead answered. "Harvey will come back to check on you after she drops me off." She gave a genuine smile. "Make yourself at home. Mercy will be by in ten or fifteen."

Both women left, but instead of a quiet room, I was met with the shrill sound of electronics sizzling in my brain. I winced, desperate for something to take the discomfort away, but settling for the glass of water waiting for me.

A text buzzed through my phone, something from my mother, surely. I swallowed the water with a hard gulp. Through blurred vision, the words were too fuzzy to make out, forcing another wave of nausea to rise up through my body from the effort.

My body was hot, yet I felt cold. My brain was sleepy, but I was wired, comfortable in this plushy couch, yet completely unsettled in my very bones. I closed my eyes and let out a labored exhale, feeling out of shape and breathless from just that sip of water.

I must have napped again. I was unsure for how long, though, since I hadn't looked at a clock in a while. It must have been the jiggling of the doorknob that brought me back. I tensed, waiting for whoever to come in from the other side. Big round eyes met mine, softening at the corners where a few lines creased.

"Erm, hi." She waved with one hand, peeking through the crack she'd made before coming in all the way and closing the door behind her. "I'm Me—"

"Mercy?" I blurted out, my nerves always beating me to the punch.

"Meredith, but yeah, Mercy on the rink. You hit your head?" She gestured to her own, pointing at the very spot that was poorly bandaged on mine.

She had blue eyes and shoulder-length, shiny black hair. Freckles splattered over just the top of her nose, and with her heels, she was probably about six feet tall, towering over me.

"That's what they said," I sighed. "And that's what the gash says too," I added with annoyance.

She fisted the first aid kit in her hands a little tighter, her lips going into a tight line before she took a step toward me. "You sure I can't convince you to go to a hospital? Stitches without any anesthesia is a real bitch." Her right eyebrow lifted, waiting for my decision.

I shook my head. I was sitting upright now, and she took the cushion to my left, propping the first aid kit on the coffee table and taking out the bare essentials.

"I'm drowning in medical debt. At this point, death would be the economical choice," I joked, forcing a snort from her.

"I hear that." She bit a smile back before digging through the side of my head and making a backward hiss when she exposed the certainly-still-bleeding wound. "Are you *sure*?" she emphasized. "It's gotta be at least four stitches."

"I can handle it," I lied, shrugging my shoulders like a boxer preparing to go a round.

"Want a towel to bite on, princess?" Harvey's voice sent a prickle down my spine, all the tiny hairs standing on command.

"I didn't realize you were back." For some reason, they were the only words that made sense to say.

"You were so peaceful sleeping." The corner of her lips tugged up.

"She's concussed," Meredith said through gritted teeth.

"I'm fine. I'm not even nauseous." I waved off the unnecessary worrying.

Harvey walked to the small kitchen. Her platinum blonde hair was shaved near her ears and the back, a fade that got longer as it came up the top, where finger length hair fell into her eyes, draping to the side. It was the kind of haircut that accentuated her jawline, making me wish I was brave enough to try something like that.

I'd worn my hair long my whole life.

Extending her tattooed arm my way, revealing a sort of Miyazaki themed sleeve, she pushed the kitchen towel in my direction, not waiting for me to confirm whether I'd need it.

"Thanks." I took it anyway, my eyes going to the scorpion tattoo on the top of her hand. It was dark, fully colored, with shades of blue and black bringing the creature damn near to life.

"That looks brutal." She winced, staring at my head.

"I think I'm gonna need to cut a bit of the hair over here," Meredith let me know before promptly taking the first aid kit scissors to a section of my hair and cutting it close to the scalp. She threw the clump of long hair onto the ground like it wasn't years of work.

"Ah!" I gasped, more out of alarm than actual pain.

"If that was bad, you're not gonna make it through this." Meredith laughed, her nickname of Mercy seeming more and more like an ironic play on her caregiving style.

I held back any display of discomfort or pain when she cleaned the wound with iodine and removed all the dried blood in the area.

I was good at pretending not to be in pain.

While my physical injuries were very real, it didn't mean I was allowed the comfort of showing that pain. My mother never failed to remind me that worse afflictions existed, and it was my job to be grateful I didn't have it worse. Because we could always have it worse.

Should have been the damn PR slogan for immigrants.

"I'm fine," I promised myself more than anyone else. "Just do it." I placed the twisted towel into my mouth, biting harder than I'd ever done in my life the minute the first needle pierced through my skin.

"Do you need a hand to hold?" Mercy asked just as Harvey plopped next to me on the couch, the outside of her bare thigh touching mine.

Mumbling around the towel before resigning to a nod, I let out a pathetic sound, grabbing the palm Harvey extended in offering.

I squeezed with the next puncture of the needle, feeling

the sensation of the thread sliding through and squirming as it pulled the skin together again.

"Not so bad?" Meredith asked.

A bead of sweat was forming at the side of my head, and I was clenching Harvey's hand so tightly, her fingertips were purple. She pulled her lips into a flat line as she snuck a quick look my way, like she was holding on to my secret, not bothering to call me out when I nodded the lie.

Each puncture was worse than the last, the pain an annoying burn, but the feeling of the thread through my flesh, through my *head*, was an unbearable agony I couldn't dissociate from. I couldn't find that happy place to go no matter how hard I gripped Harvey's hand and closed my eyes. My stomach fluttered with the pull of the thread, the mental image of my scalp being sewn shut too much to bear to block out.

"I think I'm going to throw up," I admitted just as Meredith finished the last suture, hot lava churning inside me.

Despite fighting back, the sensation wouldn't ease. Though she was already done, the feeling played on repeat long after she put away the first aid kit. Saliva pooled in the back of my mouth, my jaw burning in antici-pation of the vomit I wasn't going to be able to swallow back down.

"You shouldn't get up—" Before the kind nurse could finish, Harvey had already gotten off the couch and somehow jumped over the back of it, a trash can in hand.

"Spew," she commanded, and like a trained dog, I obeyed, opening my mouth and letting go of the latte I'd drank on the way to the rink. Thank God I hadn't managed to devour my snake meal for the day. Otherwise, it would have been twice as disgusting.

Liquid puke was fine, barely gross, especially to seasoned derby girls who were accustomed to exercise-induced nausea from skating too hard. But chunks?

At a stranger's house?

Not forgivable.

Electric chair.

With one last heave, I threw up the rest of the liquid in my stomach before letting out a pathetic groan and wiping my mouth with the back of my sweater. Relief and exhaustion hit me all at once, and I gave in, adjusting to lay down on the couch. Harvey caught me by the shoulders, eyes bulging like she just kept me from falling off a cliff.

Oh, the stitches. I *almost* forgot.

"Thanks," I released a tired smile.

My phone buzzed, a reminder that reality lived outside these apartment walls.

And I was in a stranger's house instead of the hospital in order to avoid a bill.

"Shit, I'm sorry. I'm literally just squatting in..." I looked between the two of them before remembering her name was Nadine, and she wasn't even here.

"Don't sweat it. Nadine's place is basically everyone's second home. We all have a key," Mercy assured me.

"Still, I should go. She doesn't need to deal with me when she gets home from work." I looked around for my things, but all I seemed to have was my phone.

Mercy stuck her hand out for it. "Let me put my number in there, just in case you need anything."

I hesitated. She'd done too much already, but I really

couldn't afford another medical bill right before I had to sign this new lease.

I handed it over.

"We should call a tow for your car. I can take you home if you need," Harvey offered, pulling out her phone.

"You've already done so much. I can call a cab." I shook my head, thumbing my phone for the ride-share app.

"How 'bout you pay me back by skating with us... when you're healed up, of course," Harvey bargained with a cheshire grin, one eyebrow cocked so high that it threatened to merge with her hairline.

"No deal. I'm just passing through." I pushed off the couch to stand, but my vision wavered, and everything spun again.

Harvey gripped my forearm, steadying me with one hand behind my back to keep me from falling. For a split second, my vision blackened and a hazy film draped over everything. I blinked my eyes back open.

"Maybe you should stay put. Someone should watch you tonight." Her eyebrows furrowed, the green of her eyes a clear-cut emerald with speckles of silver.

"I-I can't ask anymore of you all. I'm grateful, but no." I held back from shaking my head, knowing it would only make me dizzier. Her grip on my arm didn't loosen.

"Let me drive you then, make sure you don't pass out in the cab and get taken advantage of. There's some real weirdos in Devil Town." Her voice was low and soft, almost like a plea.

"Sure," I agreed, reaching for my phone before moving toward the door. "Thank you, Meredith." I turned back to the angel who saved me.

"Mercy, if you come skate with us." She grinned encouragingly.

I rolled my eyes, a playful smile still on my face as I reached for the doorknob, but finding Harvey already there, holding it open for me. She was still in her derby clothes, like she'd spent all day too busy taking care of Nadine's needs—my needs, as if she was someone who'd go above and beyond to ignore their own desires to satiate another's.

Dangerous.

The wrong person always took advantage of someone like her.

She stayed close, one hand always an inch from me in case I slipped on the ice while we walked down the second-floor stairs outside the apartment building. I didn't remember the walk up, but then again, maybe I hadn't walked at all. Harvey pulled her phone out and made a call. I tuned out to the quiet crunching of the snow beneath our feet to give her privacy, her hand still a hairline from catching me if I fell.

I was disoriented, not feeling myself, but also knowing I'd taken way harder hits in the past and came out fine. It was just another concussion. The jingling of her keys got my attention, her phone tucked back into her pocket as she opened her car door for me and then slid into the driver's seat.

"Your car is being towed to East End Garage. I can take you there tomorrow." She gripped the wheel and put the car in reverse before pulling out of the parking lot.

"You're being extremely nice." I pointed out the obvious, though what I was really asking was, *why?*

"You needed help," she said nonchalantly, "and you said

you're passing through, which means you probably don't have anyone you can call."

She was depressingly right. Once upon a time, these were my stomping grounds. I was two years old when my mother moved here to finish her first PhD. Now, I wasn't sure there was a single person who'd know my name anymore.

And maybe the ones who did would have nothing kind to say.

I owed nothing to Devil Town, and it held no debts toward me.

But still, it left its mark, and I yearned to do the same, to be more than the girl who shattered her way out of this town in shame. I didn't respond, leaning my temple on the cold glass window as she drove toward the motel I'd call home for the next few days.

I slid the key over the electronic lock, first flashing red and then green on the second try. Stumbling my way forward, I fell chest down into the comfort of the full size bed. A groan escaped me from sheer exhaustion, plus annoyance knowing it would be impossible to sleep with the pain hammering in the side of my head.

The sound of the door shutting reminded me I wasn't alone. I guess it was a good thing she was here; anyone could have come through the open door behind me. I was too out of it to think clearly, and it was obvious my decision-making skills were impaired. Whining, I lifted my head up slightly to look back at her.

"You look pathetic. Can I help?" She arched that eyebrow again.

I managed a grunt from the depths of my chest.

"What do you need?" She dropped to her knees so she was face to face with me splattered on the bed.

"I'm fine," I lied, not even knowing where to begin.

Everything hurt.

"You can go." Internally, I castigated myself, but I couldn't demand any more kindness from this stranger.

"I'm pretty sure if I go, you'll wake up in the middle of the night and bump your head again and die." She pulled at my coat sleeve, and I didn't bother to protest, slightly lifting my shoulders to help the process. She moved to my feet, where she carefully worked the laces of my boots, undoing them slowly, her eyes staring straight through me.

I groaned, but it wasn't enough to fight off the stranger from touching my damp socks, removing them one at a time, like she wasn't grossed out by my boot-locked feet.

I'd done nothing to deserve the kindness, and I wasn't sure I could pay it back in the way she seemed to want. I wasn't a skater anymore. I certainly wasn't a *team player* anymore.

Her phone rang, and she hopped up like a prepared alarm, glancing at it with a frown before looking my direction. "I'll be right back." She made her way outside, already answering the call with a dry, "What?" before shutting the door behind her.

I tapped the pads of my fingers to the side of my head, just skirting the area around the source of the throbbing. I was too afraid to touch it, certainly too afraid to go look at it, though I knew I needed to. I had to wash the day off me so I could start failing all over again tomorrow. My phone buzzed once more.

My mother, no doubt.

I'd deal with her in the morning, when I could think more clearly, when my brain wasn't throbbing. I couldn't wait to hear how this would never have happened if I'd just skated like she'd told me to.

She was great at that, the hindsight lessons.

Only ever reserved for me.

I'm speaking as your mother, not your therapist.

And when I needed a mother, I seemed to always find the therapist instead.

Annoyance rose to the surface, and I rolled my way out of the bed, giving myself a moment to be sure I wasn't going to fall over before hobbling to the bathroom. My ribs were sore, and my good knee didn't feel so great either, but nothing felt critical, and that was enough for me.

Good knee. Who was I kidding? They were both shit, but the one without the metal screws keeping it together was the preferred one.

Once in the bathroom, I shuffled the rest of my clothes off, avoiding the mirror as I passed, keeping my head down and dragging myself into the shower.

That was the byproduct of having seen my body in a messed-up, horrific, mangled version of itself. It was priority number one to avoid witnessing a similar image again. Even now, five years later, while avoiding the creation of a new memory for my mental filing cabinet of trauma, I could still see the picture burned into the back of my eyelids when I blinked.

My left leg, broken backwards at the knee, held together solely by the netting of my fishnet tights. My right leg twisted off to the side, but my foot pointed in a completely different direction, the weight of the skate keeping my foot firmly in place.

I braced myself on the wall and shuddered the memory away, taking a few deep breaths before dropping the final pieces of clothing to the floor and turning on the water. I was sore all over, and despite the water pressure being abhorrently low, it still beat far too violently against my bruised body.

The water was tepid when I came to, only barely making out the sound of knocking against the bathroom door. I mumbled, too groggy to care to raise my voice when the knocking came again.

I closed my eyes once more.

My skin was cold, still wet from the shower that no longer battered against my frame, when a warm towel wrapped around me. My teeth chattered, and though I mentally commanded my body to stop, I held no control over it anymore.

"I wasn't sure whether to give you privacy or break the door down," Harvey said nervously, lifting me to my feet and shouldering most of my weight.

I barely got out a "Huh?" before turning my head to find the broken door, the wood splintered in the middle where she'd used something to break through it.

"I freaked out when you didn't answer. There was no one at the front desk, and I started thinking maybe you fell and hit your head again, and that it was gonna be my fault, so I kind of just she-hulked my way in." She shrugged, helping me back to bed.

"Thanks, I think." I was too embarrassed to say anything else, so I resorted to my default settings. "You can go now. You don't have to stay."

"If I leave now, I'll *definitely* be liable for your death." She laughed at her own joke. "Why do you keep rejecting help?"

"I don't like being a burden," I admitted dryly.

"Who said you were being a burden?" Harvey asked, gently scooping up the hair behind me and running her fingers through it to detangle whatever rat's nest I was left with after the haircut Meredith gave me.

"You're telling me you'd rather be taking care of a stranger who willingly chose to forfeit a hospital in order to save a few dollars instead of doing whatever it is you'd probably be doing tonight if it weren't for me?" I lifted my head back to look at her, waiting for her response.

"I'd be drinking." The words were barely audible.

"And you don't want to drink?" I asked.

"All I want is to drink." She paused, sucking something imaginary from her teeth before continuing. "Lonnie says if I can't bout sober, I'm off the squad," she said, like the words themselves were the burden, not me.

"That bad?" I asked, knowing we were heading into delicate territory. Prying into this girl's personal demons, getting to know her, wasn't my intention, but here we were. As long as it kept the focus off me.

She shrugged. "Everything is just a lot, all the time." She scratched at her head for a split second before continuing, "I'm just constantly overstimulated, and whatever I can use to dull out the sensation of the entire universe at my back helps a little."

She sounded just like me.

"Except you're a bad drunk and nobody likes a bad drunk." I rolled to my good side, not judging, just stating plainly.

"I'm a great drunk." She crossed her arms. "As long as no one is in my way." Her tone was cocky again, as if she was proud of herself, and I couldn't help but crack a smile.

"Let me braid your hair for you, get it out of your way so it doesn't stick to the fresh stitches," she offered.

I responded with a simple nod, and she reached over me, pulling herself onto the bed and straddling my hips, holding up most of her own weight instead of resting it on my back.

Cold fingers trailed over my neck and carefully gathered all the hair still left on my head. Delicately weaving the dark strands back and forth, she pulled the braid to the side so it would avoid hitting the fresh wound. She then slipped a hairband from her wrist onto the ends of my hair before letting out a satisfied sigh.

"Thank you," I managed out. I kept my lips pressed to the mattress as I spoke, my words muffled, "You're *suspiciously* nice."

"This isn't a horror movie." She walked toward the curtains, closing them and quickly turning her head back my way. "Or is it?" she said dramatically, a mischievous grin on her face.

"You're a bad villain." My cheek was pressed to the mattress now as I watched her walk my way.

Her lips parted like she was going to reply, but her

attention went to her phone vibrating in her hand. A frown grew over her face. "I didn't want to leave you alone, but I have to go. Are you going to be okay?"

"I'm over the worst of it. Thanks for everything." My performance wasn't award-winning, but it seemed like whoever was on the other end of those texts needed her more than I did.

"O-oh okay." She fumbled with her jacket awkwardly before tossing it on. "Take care then." Her voice was flat, the frown still on her face.

My phone vibrated next. I turned my head, surprised it was still on, but it was propped up on the charger. She had set it up for me. By the time I opened my mouth to thank her, she was already gone.

I chewed on my lip, for no reason other than to draw pain elsewhere.

Something to distract from my head.

It probably wouldn't have killed me to make a friend. I'd be stuck here until I could manifest another car from the ashes of the old one. Mine was trashed; I hadn't even had a chance to examine it, but I knew the damage was beyond repair. If I blinked, I could still see the tree inches from my face, buried into the engine, the hood crumpled around it. I gripped the sheets beneath me, bracing for the impact of the airbag once more.

It never came, but when the bead of sweat dropped from my temple, I knew I had one more thing to add to my therapy rotation.

I wasn't stuck here, but now, I'd have to fly to New York, which would be a good bit more expensive than the nineteen hours of road I had planned for. I grabbed my phone, swiping past the thirteen missed calls from my mother and opening my bank app.

Three hundred, twenty-two dollars and sixteen cents. Not even enough for my apartment deposit I forgot to pay. I turned the screen off and flipped it upside down on the nightstand, not bothering to check for flights. Maybe I *was* stuck here.

My phone buzzed again.

I let out a frustrated exhale, the kind weighed down by all that came with knowing I'd disappointed my immigrant mother again. I answered, keeping the phone on the bed and hitting the speaker.

"Why aren't you answering, Antônia?" The snap in her tone let me know she'd had it with me.

I could lie, try and salvage what I could out of this, maybe figure out a way to borrow enough money to get to New York before she met me there next week.

The truth wasn't an option.

Somewhere along the way, my mother had become both my best friend and my enemy. Lying was second nature, easier than the truth, and it somehow always slipped out of my mouth first.

Because my truths were always a disappointment.

"I was showering... in my hotel." I did what I did best: gave her fractions of the truth to ease my guilt.

There was a long pause.

She was deciding whether or not she was going to turn the phone call in a different direction, or focus on the possibility of catching me lying.

"If you aren't going to skate, I expect you'll be leaving in the morning then?" The sharpness was still there, all the bite in the sentence meant to say one and one thing only.

Grow up.

Move on with your life.

"Probably," I lied my face off, knowing damn well I didn't even have a way out of this hotel, much less this town. "I need to meet up with Lonnie. For old time's sake."

"Call me once you've left the Midwest." She hung up without any formalities or familial intimacy.

Crap.

I slid down the bed, settling into the pillow and staring at the bright screen of my phone. My headache was disappearing surprisingly fast, and a quick glance at the nightstand showed me Harvey had readied my next dosage of painkillers with a glass of water poured beside them.

It took far too long to type it out, but with one eye shut and the other laser focused, I managed to send the text to Lonnie:

CAN I SEE YOU TOMORROW? I NEED A FAVOR...

The reply came almost immediately, a reassuring blanket draping me at the knowledge I would always have Lonnie to count on. I closed my eyes and crashed before I could send a response or even a thanks.

"**I**'m offended you thought you had to take a cab to my place. You know I would have sent one of the skaters to get you." Lonnie poured the hot water from the kettle into two teacups, the bags already positioned and ready.

"*I know,*" I said with all the attitude of the twenty-year-old they once knew. "Don't you realize that's half the problem?" I feigned outrage. "You have these girls moving all around Devil Town, running your errands for you. I don't need any of them meeting me under the conditions of assuming I'm important enough for a chauffeur." I shook my head, taking the teacup by the saucer plate.

Lonnie chuckled. "No, you don't want them realizing you *are* important enough for a chauffeur. Like it or not, you're still hot shit around this place."

Still shaking my head, I stirred the teabag around in the hot water bath, the string entwining around the spoon handle. "I'm no one, Lonnie. Just some girl with a bunch of pins in her leg and some crazy stories I'll never live up to again."

"Jesus Christ, Antônia, you sound like some old timer on their deathbed. You broke your leg, *five years ago*. You had surgery, you healed. Time to get strong and kick ass again, if you ask me. Before your thirties come knocking— then it'll *really* be over." They laughed at their own morbid sense of humor, tucking the grown out gray mesh behind their ear.

Lonnie was taller than me, which wasn't an accomplishment since I was certifiably president of the short kids' club. Their hair was kept in a shoulder length shag that was now a perfect combination of salt and pepper, these days.

The oven dinged, and Lonnie stood, excitedly hopping over to it, their hand sheathed in the protective mitt. I could smell the butter oozing off the chocolate croissants, and my mouth watered, ready to bite into the crispy, flaky pastry.

"I miss doing this with your pão de queijo." They sighed, placing the pastries on a cooling rack.

"They were my mom's." I snorted, thinking back to the many heart to hearts we'd had in this very kitchen over black coffee and fresh-baked pão de queijo.

Now, Lonnie was drinking tea and baking their own croissants. Time was a moving force that waited for no one.

"I still miss those things." They shrugged.

Moaning at the first bite of the croissant, I savored the burst of flavor goodness rolling along my tastebuds, salty, chocolate, and warm. Perfection. "I don't know; these are pretty damn good." I chuckled. "When'd you start baking?"

"Not long after you cleared out." Lonnie shrugged.

"You left a big hole. We were all kind of lost. Eventually, one by one, everyone went their own way, and—"

"You stayed. All alone." I deflated with their confirming nod. "Fuck, I'm sorry, Lon." Tears welled in my eyes at the thought of Lonnie having been left here all alone the last five years.

"It made sense. I didn't blame any of them for movin' on with their lives." They paused, as if in thought. "We were a family. When you left, nothing felt right anymore."

My heart hurt. Moving on didn't feel so good after the realization that time didn't stop for those left behind.

"I hate that," I confessed, removing the tea bag and squeezing the too-hot water out of it before setting it to the side on my saucer. "They should have stayed," I said, convincing myself it wasn't my fault.

Failing.

"Everyone is dealing with their own shit. They didn't owe me nothin', Nia," Lonnie assured me, bringing the cup to their lips.

This rink had been Lonnie's dream. Together, we worked our butts off to raise the downpayment so we could all have a place to skate. Little had our crew known how badly a skate rink had been needed in Devil Town. It was a magical place where people came to skate, roller derby teams formed, and the town came alive with excitement to watch. Lonnie created a community, and together, we became closer than blood under this very roof.

Lonnie coached us four nights a week until every skater under the black and red colors of the Devil's Dames was a force to be reckoned with. Strong thighs, bruised shoulders, ripped fishnets, bloody lips. Where most teams required a skater to pass twenty-seven laps in under five minutes, the Dames required it in four.

Speed, mayhem, maximum effort.

We lived for it.

We needed it.

Because we were all lost, and it wasn't just about the skates. It was about being there for each other, about skating our anger out until we threw up, because the next best option was doing drugs behind the Qmart on a Tuesday. That was all small-town life could offer any of us who hadn't gotten out fast enough.

Lonnie saved us from that.

Lonnie saved *me* from that.

I'd wanted nothing more than to run to the streets, because anything was better than the prison of my mother's home. Home was where every mirror stood as a promise of her reflection in my future, where my debts racked up and the bookie would no doubt come to collect. Because my mother *always* collected; whether physically or emotionally, it didn't matter to her.

She'd get hers every time.

I was meant to be a trophy, a medal, a prize, but she couldn't hang me on a shelf.

I wasn't gold. I wasn't bronze, not even copper on my best days.

Maybe if I hadn't been an only child, she wouldn't have put all her eggs in one basket.

"You're not here to feel sorry for me, you're here for you. What happened yesterday? Thought you were gonna come by and skate? Instead, I'm hearing Mercy was patchin' you up on Nadine's couch?" Lonnie took a loud slurp of tea. "Where's your car?"

"You're drinking tea," I pointed out, avoiding every single one of their questions.

"The caffeine was giving me tittie lumps," they said casually between sips.

I practically spat mine out, coughing as I choked on the liquid going down the wrong pipe. "Like, cancer?" I asked.

"Nah, nothin' like that. The doctor said caffeine doesn't help. Had to cut out even the decaf. I was having the cysts drained every couple weeks. Finally decided to just stop with the crap all together." They raised the cup of herbal tea in the air, and I met it with mine, clinking them before taking a sip.

I swallowed the hot tea, letting it soothe my throat as it warmed my belly with every gulp. "Sounds like some old people shit." I slurped obnoxiously as I lifted an eye from my cup to catch Lonnie's reaction.

"Old is my foot in your ass, you little brat. Are you gonna tell me what happened to your car yet?" they pressed, scratching the thick, wavy head of hair on their head.

I sighed, far too dramatically, but annoyed at myself to even be in this position.

"My mom." I'd barely said the words, and Lonnie was already shaking their head and chuckling. They knew our history was stickier than the gum stuck to the bottom of the bleachers at a bout. "No. It wasn't my mom." I took account-ability for my own bullshit, knowing damn well had I been a big girl and just not taken the call, I wouldn't have been so distracted, wouldn't have hit the tree.

It wasn't my mom.

It was me.

I was in control of my reactions. It was up to me.

"I was distracted, the car hit a patch of ice right before Diver's bridge, and I crashed into a tree. The engine is wrecked. Probably. I don't know." I looked down, pushing the half-eaten croissant around the plate.

"You don't know?" There it was: the judging, parental look Lonnie was so good at dishing out to any of us who thought we were too big for our britches.

Lonnie never had a problem taking us down a peg and reminding us we weren't.

"I was pretty out of it. Your girls got me and handled it all. I haven't even called the garage yet," I told them.

Lonnie's arms crossed over their chest slowly, I knew I was going to hear it.

"I'm not here for lectures, Lonnie. If anything, I'm trying to escape them. I can't be a big girl if no one ever lets me," I complained, already preparing to bolt at the sign of a speech.

"You maybe think they don't let you because you keep screwing up every time you're given the chance to be an adult?" They put their cup down, the detached look on their face letting me know I couldn't Nia my way out of this one.

"Ouch, Lon." Shrinking, I leaned back into the chair, shoulders slumped.

They stared at me, both of us silent. I avoided my oldest friends' gaze as much as humanly possible, my shame over-whelming me, telling me to just get the fuck out of here, because disappointing my mother was somehow easier than disappointing "Mommy" Lonnie Green.

"You came to me. I offer truths in exchange for your shame. Now, you said you needed cash. To fix the car?" They took a sip of tea, waiting for my response.

"Forget the car. It's more trouble than it's worth to take a car to New York. I'm going to spend twice my rent just paying for parking. I just need a couple gigs so I can get a plane ticket by next week." I grinned my best sparkling white smile at them, knowing they wouldn't deny me.

No one wanted to work concessions at bouts. I was doing them a favor.

"No deal." Lonnie shook their head.

"What do you mean?" I practically shouted, knowing how absurd it was for them to turn down cheap, tax-free labor.

"Nadine's little sister works concession now. I don't need you." They smirked. "But," Lonnie held up a finger, wielding my anticipation against me, "I'll buy your ticket if you skate the next bout."

"No." I stood, scraping the chair against the wooden floors loudly as I pushed away from the table. "I can't skate, not like that. I'm not who I used to be."

"You're afraid." There was no question in their tone, no yearning for understanding. They were simply stating it as fact.

Shit.

Lonnie knew me too well, too good at seeing through me. Seeing everything.

"Of course I'm afraid, Lonnie. I spent seven months in a wheelchair and took a year to learn how to walk again! You think just because I can, that I want to risk it all again just so you can *see* if I'm really as damaged as they say?" I exploded, not able to contain the anger seeping from my very pores.

"That's a shame." Lonnie scoffed. "I thought Nia da Silva didn't quit."

"And I thought you promised to always do right by your skaters." I narrowed my eyes at them.

"You left. You're not one of mine anymore." Lonnie reached into the chest pocket of their green flannel, pulling a cigarette from the pack and lighting it in the poorly ventilated room.

The only window in here didn't open to the outside, but to the rink. This tiny apartment had been the biggest reason Lonnie bought the entire place. They needed a home, and then they made Skateland *our* home.

Apparently not mine anymore, though.

With the confirmation of their last words, I packed my bruised ego deep into the trenches of my subconscious and blinked away the excess water in my eyes before they could form into tears. If Lonnie wanted this to be transactional, I could make it transactional.

"What's the point of me skating one bout? That desperate for a win?" I masked any sign of emotion.

"I want to show them what a real jammer skates like. We're making do, subbing a few blockers here and there into jammer positions, but they aren't fast. Bunch of giraffes, skating all awkward and clunky with no grace. And yeah, we can't win. Not like this." They took a long drag of the cigarette, the ash growing with the pull.

"Fine. One bout. If you break my leg again, you're paying for my hospital bill this time, Lonnie." I clenched my jaw shut tight, hoping they'd realize what they were asking was far beyond my comfort level, far beyond what I'd ever willingly choose to do.

They nodded, a crooked smirk painted over their face.

"I mean it. You don't know what it's like to see your body look so..." The image of my broken leg flashed behind my eyelids: the compound fracture in two separate places, my foot in the wrong direction. I winced before finishing my thought. "Wrong."

"You're a big girl. Don't sign up for what you can't handle." Lonnie slurped louder.

"You're literally tying my hands behind my back, Lon," I said, grinding my teeth together in frustration.

"No, you're just the one who refuses to see it's not too late to start being honest with your mother as an option."

I cleared my throat, standing and walking my dirty dishes to the sink.

"You're a pain in the ass. I don't need a second mom again," I told them with a sigh, leaning on the sink as I took in their studio apartment.

Nothing had changed since the last time I'd been here—nothing but Lonnie. I couldn't put my finger on it, and even though I could see that everything they were saying, everything they intended, was for my benefit, for my own good, I couldn't help but feel like this wasn't the Lonnie I remembered.

"I'm no one's mom anymore," they said, sticking a toothpick into their mouth and prodding between two teeth. "Boundaries and what not. I went down hard after all you girls left, realized I was too attached playing second mommy to everyone. *Mommy Lonnie.*" They snorted. "I still have the jersey y'all made me."

I gave them the kind of look that said '*you're full of it.*' Lonnie was obsessed with their skaters; that's why we flocked to them. Because with Lonnie, you felt at home.

"I can still give sage advice and have boundaries." They didn't look at me, sipping from the teacup again.

"Fine. I'll be here tomorrow to skate," I announced, making my way to the door.

"I'll leave the backdoor open for you. Practice is at six, but you knew that." They laughed, the noise following me all the way through the rink.

I finally took a moment to admire the place. The light brown wooden floors were still waxed to perfection, just the way Lonnie demanded. Multicolored bulbs hung from strings across the rink, and on slam nights, when there were bouts, they shone in technicolor.

The popcorn stand was still covered in oil, the t-shirt booth had a few more broken boards and missing nails, and the ticket table was the same old disorganized mess: exactly the same as before. I walked across the rink in my shoes, sacrilegious, basically a crime.

But this wasn't my world anymore. I was just a passerby. A visitor. A tourist, vacationing in their land.

My fingers trailed against the railing, lazily skimming the wall as I reached the doors. But there, in my periphery, were the cubbies we crammed our belongings into in order to avoid using the locker rooms. They'd been meant for the general public, those who came and rented skates and needed somewhere to put their shoes, but with time, we all resorted to using them. I couldn't help it; I didn't have to search for it. I was automatically drawn to the one stamped with the number thirteen and the faded *Green Day* sticker still proudly glued to the frame.

The only proof I'd ever been here at all.

Tears prickled, and my vision blurred.

You will not cry here, I commanded, breathing in deeply and pushing through the front doors of the rink. The frosty bite of the winter day hit me right in the face, invading my nostrils and freezing the fresh dripping snot that came with the tears I'd fought off.

The cab was waiting, the driver scrolling through his phone when I opened the door and stepped inside. Relishing the hot blast of air from the heater, my shoulders dropped, and I relaxed for the first time in longer than I could remember.

Not because I had a plan, not because I might actually be able to pull it off, but because tomorrow, I'd be skating again. I let the smile cover my face, and I closed my eyes, leaning back before I buckled in for the ride back to the motel.

My legs had never felt weaker. I had lost all feeling below the knees from the buildup and anxiety. Even though Lonnie promised I'd have Skateland to myself for a few hours, I practically had diarrhea from the anticipation.

But here I stood, *again*, in front of the rink that made me who I was. Bag hanging from my shoulders, I walked through the double doors, this time ready. Confidence buzzed through my veins as I hunted for the number thirteen cubby, throwing my sneakers in and dropping the duffle bag full of skate crap onto the floor.

I didn't need to double check that I was alone before lowering my sweatpants, the black pantyhose underneath not alluding to any modesty. I reached into the bag, fishing out a pair of spandex shorts that probably didn't fit anymore and unrolling my socks until they were fully stretched out to the tops of my knees. Gripping the bottom of my hoodie, I slid it over my head, and then did the same with the t-shirt underneath, leaving only a sports bra.

Now for my armor.

I was opening a tomb, releasing dead parts of me that had been hiding, waiting for their day in the sun again, to give another chance for this shell of my body to live once more. That was what it felt like, to be a completely different person than the girl who used to put on these skates nearly every day and wreck her body until she had to be carried out of the track.

I thought I'd buried that girl, sealed her casket with five-inch nails.

But here she was, digging through the dirt to show her face again, wearing a satisfied smile as she crept closer to the surface with every piece of gear. First the elbow pads, then the ones for the knees before I rummaged through the bag and pulled the helmet from the bottom of it.

I smirked.

My old friend Starscreamer's *To punish and enslave* sticker from the *Transformers* movie was still there, stuck to the side, worn from time. She'd slapped that one on the very day I bought the helmet, telling me it was good luck to have it tagged by someone else first. The next day, I skated my first twenty-seven laps around the rink in under four minutes, guaranteeing my spot on the A team for the Devil's Dames derby league.

I raised the helmet above my head like a crown being placed on a monarch, and if I had any audience, I'm sure it would have been a sight to see. I buckled the strap under my chin and finally reached under the bench for the pièce de résistance.

My custom made, Quadstar carbon fiber boot roller skates with the highest quality gumdrop toe-stoppers, equipped with the fifty-nine millimeter Evolve wheels I'd finally switched them into. Seven years ago, I maxed out an entire credit card on this gear. It took me nearly two years to pay it all off, but it was worth it. I unzipped the duffle's side pocket, unleashing my three-headed, five-in-one, handy-dandy skate tool. It came with two sizes of Allen keys, two socket wrenches, and a bearing puller—everything a self-sufficient skater needed to keep their quads perfectly tuned.

I sat on the bench, ritualistically adjusting my plates and bearings, tightening everything up how I liked it, the way I had always done before a practice or a bout. I slipped one foot in at a time, lacing through each loop with a slow deliberateness, savoring every pass of the cords like it'd be the last time.

I never got to have a *last time*, not by my own plans and standards, anyway. I mean, unless you counted being carried out of the track by a six-foot-three blocker, mirroring the cover of the cult classic *The Bodyguard*. Embarrassment washed over me, forming goosebumps throughout my body from the memory.

Tying the final lace into a double loop before covering them with the Velcro protective leather, I reached back into my bag for the final piece of the puzzle: my wrist guards. The first one always went on easily on my left hand, using my dominant side to close it as tightly as it needed, but the right one was always a chore. I gripped the Velcro strap with my teeth and pulled it opposite where it stretched, tightening it before closing it.

I stood, three to four inches taller again for the first time in five years.

Taking my first step forward, I wobbled, my body

forgetting how low my center of gravity needed to be when wearing these skates.

Muscle memory, my butt.

I took a nervous breath, wondering if I'd hyped this up too much, if my body had forgotten how good we were at this.

If all of this had been for nothing.

I grabbed the railing along the wall, not picking my heavy feet up and simply pushing forward like a toddler skating for the first time. I passed by the mirror on the wall and doubled back, turning toward it.

I was too upright. It looked awkward and wrong, and I laughed at the thought of Lonnie calling their skaters clumsy giraffes. I bent my knees, taking a deep seat into my own thighs and feeling the burn in my well-rested quad muscles.

There she was.

With my center of gravity where it needed to be and the mirror reminding me exactly what a bad B looked like when she remembered who she was, I spun on my skates, one foot in front of the other, into the track.

I was so out of shape; this was going to be so ugly.

Moving against my own thoughts, I weaved one knee over the other, remembering the way each crossover should feel as I rounded the corner of the track the first time, leaning deep into my left.

Joy bubbled at my chest, unadulterated, pure bliss, commanding a wild laugh to fall free from my throat, adding to the loud sounds of my wheels dropping on the wood with each pass of my skates. I sat even lower, the burn in my thighs turning my muscles into liquid fire as I whipped faster and faster in the tight circle of the oval track.

This was freedom.

I had forgotten. *How could I forget?*

How could I have erased from my brain the thrill of *this* right here, on a track, with four wheels on each foot? I turned on my skates, moving backwards now and letting the momentum carry my body until I needed to push back.

I guess it *was* like riding a bike. Not that I ever learned to ride one.

I had been on skates since I could walk, first in-line and then, in the third grade, my father gifted me my first pair of quads. They were hot pink, with glitter all over the plastic boots.

They changed my whole world.

I forced my father to spend every afternoon in the Devil Town skatepark, watching me as I blasted through the ramps and half pipes with no regard to the skater boys doing their own things on their boards.

I was made for wheels. That was what my father had said.

That was where I met Lonnie, who taught me how to drop in, how to skate backwards, and every basic maneuver manageable on quad wheels. Eventually my dad stopped taking me to the skatepark, and instead Lonnie, who had become a family friend at that point, had earned his trust. A couple years later, the city council decided a skate park brought in "poor quality citizens" and turned it into a parking lot. Then, Lonnie became our hero, making sure anyone who wanted to skate had a place to go. By then, I had recruited all my friends onto eight wheels of their own, and Elliot Page had just starred in "Whip-it". There was only one thing left to do.

Form a roller derby league.

Lonnie killed it when it came to logistics. They were our coach, our manager, our cheerleader, our friend, and despite whatever B.S they were trying to sell me now, they were our family, and they took pride in it. I extended my arms into a T, feeling the self-made breeze as I curved the track backwards.

"Is that all you got?"

Whipping my head around to search for the voice, I stretched out, straightening my knees and throwing off my balance. Forgetting every basic roller derby skill in the book, I fell hard on my butt instead of forward onto my pads.

"Porra!" I cursed in my mother's language, my ass screaming at me from the impact of the hard floor.

Harvey laughed. *She freaking laughed.* The open mouth kind of laugh that echoed loudly in the empty rink. I frowned, more embarrassed than angry, but still feeling violated in a strange way.

"How long have you been here?" I yelled across the track, knowing my voice carried just fine without having to.

"What would you say if I said the whole time?" Harvey grinned. "Definitely for the whole crown/helmet show." She was geared up, but I hadn't seen her somehow.

"Where were you?" I narrowed my eyes further.

"I came out of the bathroom right when you dropped your pants." She shrugged, rolling into the track shoulder first. "How's your head?"

"About as good as it can feel on 800 milligrams of NSAIDs," I said flatly, watching her smooth crossovers one after the other as she lapped around me.

The back of her t-shirt read 'Harvey Dent-her-face', and the front had the Devil's Dame logo on it. Black bat-wing stickers were placed symmetrically on opposite sides of her helmet. Her footwork was graceful, smooth, precise, but she wasn't fast.

A blocker, maybe even a pivot, but definitely not a jammer.

She was on her fourth pass circling me when she turned on her wheels, skating backwards and tightening her circle so she was even closer as she wound around me. "I thought I had the track to myself," I admitted.

"There's a ninety nine percent chance you're never alone in Skateland," she said, her right hand gripping her left wrist behind her back.

"Yeah, but that's because Lonnie lives here." I rolled my eyes. "They said I'd have the rink to myself before practice." I didn't bother to hide my annoyance.

I wanted at least an hour to myself, to get to know my body on skates again before I'd have some sort of audience.

"No, they didn't." She shook her head, and I opened my mouth to argue, but then I remembered she was right. They actually didn't. I simply told Lonnie I'd be coming, assuming I'd have the space to myself.

I sighed, frustrated yet still attempting to console my brain with the change of plans. I didn't enjoy last minute surprises. I needed the reliability. The constant guarantee of the predictable.

Don't you think you're a little too old to spiral so hard from a blip in your routine?

My mother's voice found the back of my conscience, but I pushed it down, drowning it under the sound of Harvey's quads hitting the track with each crossover.

"Come on, you looked good out here. Quick on your feet," she antagonized. "Let's see what you got, superstar."

The grin was borderline malicious.

"You're mocking me." I told her. "I never hyped myself up. I don't think I'm anything special," I reassured her.

"They do." She gestured to Lonnie's door with her forehead. "So I wanna see for myself."

"I'm rusty," I reminded her, my insecurities wrapping around me like a symbiote, slithering up my extremities before it devoured me whole.

"I'm not asking for footwork drills; just a couple laps to warm up before the rest of the team gets here." She sounded so reasonable, but her final words had me doubling back.

The rest of the team.

I'd have to face the judgment of all of them, and now, Lonnie had placed me so high up a pedestal, they were expecting some fairy-tale version of the girl I had once been. The girl I had no way of being again.

I was good because I was reckless, which was the one thing I couldn't be anymore. I couldn't skate like I didn't care about getting hurt, because I would always be hyper aware. I would always be afraid of the wrong move, waiting to catch a misstep so I could lessen the damage.

It was the reality of my trauma. I would never get to skate freely again, because I would *always* carry the fear of getting hurt again. Nothing would erase that.

"Five laps," I told her, knowing if I backed out, it would look bad for Lonnie and the faith they had put in me.

I could skate five laps.

I hadn't even stretched. I wasn't prepared to give a hundred percent when all I'd meant to do was feel my skates beneath me again. I wasn't ready, but here this girl was, knowing exactly which buttons to push to get me to do what she wanted.

The red tape line on the track was vivid, like Lonnie had repainted it recently. Knees bent, raised up on our toe-stops, our bodies side by side like a perfect mirrored reflection, we got into position. She was built like a blocker, every muscle honed to defend, but her stance was for speed. Had she been skating as their jammer out of pure necessity? I turned my head forward, focusing on the track three feet ahead of me.

She counted down:

Three

Two

One

We moved. One knee passed the other in a perfect rhythm. I did what I did in every bout and focused on her body, on her speed. I had to make it a race, or I would lose every time. If I zeroed in on her body, I gave myself a goal, a marker to beat.

I always came out the victor.

If I focused only on myself, I pushed too hard and always got hurt.

She laughed behind me, the heavy clunks of her wheels following with every forceful pass of her feet. Her presence was massive behind me, and I knew that while she'd struggle to catch up to me, I'd be screwed if she did. One hit would send me across the track.

I heard a whistle in the distance, and on command, my body responded, my skates turning 180 degrees so I could come to a derby stop. Lonnie stood in front of their apartment door, clapping, a ridiculous grin on their face. Only when in front of me did Harvey come to a stop.

"She's fast, right?" Lonnie asked her.

"Too bad she doesn't wanna skate for you." Harvey chuckled, wiping sweat off her forehead with the back of her arm.

"It's not like that. I'm just passing through." I shook my head.

She closed the distance between us in two or three passes, stopping right in front of me with narrowed eyes. "You keep saying that like it's the only excuse you have." She didn't let me respond before she turned away, skating towards Lonnie like she hadn't just knocked me down a peg.

This girl could get under my skin, I knew it. She was pushy, aggressive, sarcastic as hell, and exactly the kind of friend I would have been looking for five years ago. Except I wasn't looking for friends anymore.

I was just looking for a fresh start, and the grave where all my traumas were buried wasn't exactly the best garden for new beginnings.

"I thought I'd have the rink to myself." I attempted to fight back my stinkface at Lonnie.

"Never said that. No one ever has the rink to themselves anymore. Tough luck, Nia." They shrugged, leisurely walking across the track toward the locker rooms.

No sooner had they said the words did the front doors swing open. Three girls with duffel bags slung over their backs laughed loudly to something a fourth girl had said behind them. A rush of nostalgia flooded my senses, an overwhelming sense of sadness, like I was viewing my past life through some sort of out-of-body experience. My legs turned to gelatin under me, my spine becoming soft spaghetti, all my courage ready to come out of me as nervous vomit.

My feet were stones beneath me, and suddenly, the discomfort of my skates, too tightly laced around my socks, was the only thing I had any sensory awareness of. I swallowed a hard gulp, turning into a paler statue of myself as I watched more skaters file into the gym, all with a comfortable familiarity that screamed of me being the outsider.

I despised that feeling; it was all I had felt for the last five years, skirting through university like a lone wolf with no desire for a pack. It was a filthy lie—the pack was all I craved, all I wanted and everything I needed.

It was what every kid who didn't feel whole from their God-given family needed, what we were desperate for, what brought us together, despite whatever our circumstances and upbringing may have been. We craved love, connection, support. Roller derby gave us that.

The only person I recognized was Mo, who looked happy to wave me over into the slew of skaters they were rounding up.

"Glad to see you changed your mind!" they shouted over the loud-talking skaters, drawing the attention of everyone in the room and pointing directly at me.

"Crap." I couldn't keep it inside.

"You thought you were gonna skate past practice without anyone noticing you? Come on!" Harvey bumped shoulders with me before skating ahead, her bellow echoing through the rink.

"Fresh meat!" she hollered, the rest of them stomping their heavy skates on the floor in the rhythm of *"we will, we will rock you"* like the tradition had never once dimmed. If my stomach had anything inside, it would have probably leaked in either direction from nerves.

Fresh meat?

Never once in my life had I been considered *fresh meat*. Sure, I had to pay my dues just like any other skater, pass all my footwork requirements and my speed test, but *never* had I been labeled *fresh meat*. Everyone who once knew me knew I had founded this place from the ground up with Lonnie, that my fingerprints were still stamped onto the concrete walls in the bathroom from when we patched a hole in the still-abandoned building.

But everyone who once knew me was now gone.

I sighed, hanging my head as I shamefully accepted the title, knowing it was irrelevant now. It didn't matter to them, it wouldn't matter to Lonnie anymore, and it certainly didn't keep me from leaving them five years ago.

The only way to shake it would be to prove myself.

I followed behind Harvey, practically crashing into the overly excited gaggle of skaters measuring me up and down while simultaneously bombarding me with thousands of questions. Some were directed at me, some at Lonnie.

"This is the jammer?"

"Lonnie says you're back in town just to skate with us?"

"We are gonna murder those West Town Dollies this weekend with you!"

"Is your leg okay now?"

Lonnie blew a whistle, quieting the hoard. "Warm up, Devils." It was the only instruction needed. The pack broke apart, finding their place in a uniform line as they took their warmup laps. I moved to follow, but Lonnie gripped my wrist.

I looked back. "I've talked you up to my girls real good, Nia. Don't let me down; don't let *them* down," they confessed.

"As long as you didn't promise more than I'm willing to give, Lonnie. One game," I reminded them through clenched teeth.

"I know you, Nia. All you need is that first win under you. You're an addict." They threw me a knowing wink.

I shook my head, more to rattle their words out of my mind, as if they could somehow slip through my ears without my brain registering them. I didn't need the complication of how right they were.

I didn't need the fear of knowing Devil Town had such a vise grip on me that all it would take was the smell of rubber wheels against this track to pull me back in. I raised up on my toe stops, bending my front knee to ready myself for a sprint so I could catch up with the pack.

"Hold on there, turbo." Lonnie pulled me back in. "You can skate, you can practice, but you can't scrimmage."

"What the hell!? What gives, Lonnie? *You* asked me here. What's the point of throwing me into a bout if you won't let me practice scrimmage first?" I crossed my arms, flaring my nostrils in anger.

"Not yet, Nia. I learned my lesson. No fresh meat on the track until you pass your skills, which I *know* you can do. *With practice.* Take the next couple days to get your skates under you again. Relax. Fall a little, will you?" They chuckled.

"I'm not good at being the new girl on the block, especially when I know the block like the back of my hand," I groaned, frustrated at my circumstances.

"The block doesn't recognize you anymore. Get to know it again. All these skaters are dyin' to meet you, Nia, to learn from you." They nodded their head toward the perfect line of skaters making their second or third lap of their warmups.

"I have nothing to teach them." I threw my hands up in defense, laughing at the suggestion. "Unless they want to learn how to recover from multiple compound fractures, then I'm your girl."

"Stop selling yourself short. You're fast, you take the right risks, and you've got the cleanest crossovers I've ever seen to date *still*. I'm not trying to knock you down a peg by asking you to take your skills test; I'm just protecting myself." Lonnie shook their head, pulling a folded piece of paper out of their back pocket and handing me a pen. "Sign this, would you?"

"Is this..." I look over the fine print briefly. "A waiver?" I laughed. "This is seriously about protecting your ass?"

"Look, when Hank carried you out of the rink, my first thought was, 'Did I just ruin that girl's life?'" they confessed.

"Lonnie—"

"No. Listen. My second thought was, '*I'm* ruined.' I thought for sure I'd see you back here with your mom, threatening to sue me to death because I never had you sign any sort of waiver. I was scared, but I learned my lesson. I gotta protect myself too." They pushed the pen in my face.

I grabbed it.

"I get it," I sighed, using Lonnie's back as a surface to sign.

"Skate some laps, warm up and do some drills. Tomorrow is another day you're closer to, what was it you wanted again? *A new start?*" Lonnie snorted, fanning their arm out in the direction of the pack.

The sooner I took my skills test, the better. I didn't need one more thing messing with the delicate balance of my so-called confidence.

I moved obediently, doing my best to blend into the queue of skaters and move just slower than the slowest in the pack. I wasn't here to show off; I was here to skate, and if the universe was on my side, win a bout. Then, I'd get my ticket home and prevent disappointing the matriarch while checking off every item on my list on the way.

Not bad for a total shit show.

I was dragging my skates. Fast was only good enough with the stamina to maintain it, and being five years off my game, my stamina was nonexistent. I forgot what a hardass Lonnie was when it came to coaching, and spending the first twenty minutes of practice running laps had my thighs burning under me.

Mo readied the drills, finally introducing themselves to me as the assistant coach. Their name was Morgan, but the back of their shirt said Mad Mo. They put each cone down, setting up ladders side by side in two rows so that each skater transitioned from warm up laps directly into a line.

I dropped my hands to my knees, snow plowing my way to the line but sliding past my water bottle, scooping it up just to squirt a splash of water on my face. Gasping for air, I did my best to play it cool, but I knew there was no way I was living up to any of these skaters' *former derby star* dreams Lonnie had planted into their brains.

I was just a girl who broke her leg five years ago and knew some fancy footwork.

And I was starting to think I couldn't handle keeping my end of the bargain.

What if this was a huge mistake? What if I got hurt again?

My feet ached beneath me, a scorching heat radiating at the torture of wearing tight skates again for the first time in years. I'd been on my feet for two hours now, way past quitting time for someone who was breaking themselves in again.

"Not thinking of giving up yet, are you?" Mo taunted as they placed the last cone down.

"I can barely feel my legs anymore," I gasped, still struggling to catch my breath. "You'll need a wheelbarrow to get me home if I push through it," I admitted, knowing well that it was my all or nothing attitude that tended to get me in situations where I got hurt.

Thankfully, my head was just a dull throb now, easily manageable with a handful of over-the-counter pain pills.

"You killed it out there. Don't let Mo bully you into overdoing it. Go take your skates off and stretch," Harvey commanded like she had any authority.

Maybe she did. By the looks of it, she was probably captain. My eyes trailed to the shiny fabric hanging from her back pocket, the pivot helmet panty that designated her position, the dark stripe in the middle too prominent to miss.

"Nia-Death doesn't quit," Lonnie announced.

It shouldn't have gotten to me like it did, but Lonnie knew exactly where my buttons were and what it took to push them. I rolled my shoulders back, cracked my neck to the right and then the left side without my hands, took a deep breath, and rose to my toe-stops. I looked down at my feet, and then my gaze floated up to the tattooed blonde eyeing me with curious suspicion.

Harvey.

All my thoughts cleared, and suddenly, the need to prove anything disappeared.

My shoulders dropped, and I skated off the track, waving back at Lonnie. "Not anymore, Lon. I'm not that girl."

I couldn't be *all-or-nothing-Nia* anymore. I couldn't be the girl who took any challenge as long as it meant proving someone wrong. My legs thanked me, practically giving out the moment my wheels hit the worn-out carpet that still coated every inch of the rink outside of the flat track.

The retro blue and green triangle pattern was so filthy, it was hard to distinguish between the two colors, making it impossible to see the shapes at all. I dropped to it, extending my legs out in front of me and not giving any second thought as I laid my back down and finally filled my lungs with deep, full breaths.

A few minutes went by before I finally sat up again, bringing my feet in and working to unlace my skates. Was I bitching out? I hated the feeling of not giving my all. What was the difference between your all and too much? Five years later, I still wasn't sure, and while there was a drop of pride in drawing a line, in telling myself enough was enough and there wasn't anyone's validation I needed, I was still ashamed.

Humiliated I wasn't strong enough to do the things I could once do and embarrassed I couldn't keep up with practiced skaters. I kicked myself internally, ignoring every tool in my metaphorical toolbox I'd worked so hard in therapy to create as a weapon against my intrusive thoughts. I knew I wasn't weak; I knew I was doing the logical thing, the *smart* thing, in order to preserve my body if I was *actually* going to make it to skating the bout on Saturday.

Four days.

I had four more days. There was no chance in hell I was going to get in shape in four days. Three, not counting the bout day.

I looked back at the track; the skaters were now finishing their footwork drills and moving on to position for scrimmage. Harvey pulled the stripe from her back pocket and handed it to a girl I didn't recognize, grabbing the star from Lonnie's hand and slipping it over her helmet.

Interesting.

I removed my skates slower than ever before, my eyes glued on the blonde jammer handing another star to Nadine. They stood shoulder to shoulder, waiting for Lonnie to blow the whistle. The blockers got into position behind their line, two solid teams forming for the scrimmage as Mo threw yellow fishnet vests to half the skaters and one of the jammers.

The whistle blew, Nadine darting past the line with an impressive hip check as she threw Harvey off balance and split the gap between them. She moved, one skate in front of the other, pounding the track, never once looking back to see how far behind Harvey was.

She was right on Nadine's heels, and it took a simple wide turn on the next curve to get Harvey in the lead, and one shove of her right shoulder against Nadine's left had her sliding off the boundaries of the track on her ass. She took far too long to bounce back, to hop on her toe stops and find her way back to the pack.

The jam was clearly Harvey's, who was too far ahead for Nadine to catch up to even with a miracle at this point. Harvey brought her hands to her hips, signaling the end of the jam and forcing Lonnie to blow the whistle.

Not bad.

I stretched my toes, picking the sweaty lint stuck in the webbing as two more jams played out. Nadine and Harvey took turns winning, as if neither was significantly more skilled or faster than the other so it truly depended on the luck of the circumstances of the jam.

Those were the hardest.

Being evenly matched with someone in speed, strength, and skills meant the jam, the entire bout, could go in any direction. It meant a single misstep could lose you everything.

I thought back to that day with Reese-Ender, how we'd been going toe to toe for two years every few weeks, how the Wolverines were guaranteed to win a match unless they were facing us. Then, it was a gamble, simply up to fate, up to footwork.

I walked all the way around the track, my finger grazing the top of the partition wall until I made it to the other side, where the locker room entrance stood. It looked like rarely anyone still used these showers. I didn't enjoy staying in sweaty clothes, even if it was just for a short ride home. The feeling of sweat cooling and drying on my clothes, turning my skin into fire from the unbearable itch of it as it rubbed against me, was one I couldn't tolerate. I dropped my clothes to the ground in the bathroom, grabbing my toiletries from my duffel bag and turning the nozzle of the shower on.

The skaters were filing out of the track and undoing their gear on the benches by the time I'd made my way out of the showers. I was terrible at removing myself from a room, always too awkward to know if it even mattered if I said goodbye, if anyone would even notice me leave. One thing was always guaranteed, though: after leaving, I'd ruminate on how rude it was that I ghosted my way out.

It was my legacy.

All my things stuffed into my gym bag, I slung it over my shoulder and walked past the line of skaters on the bench, averting my eyes and keeping my gaze forward out of sheer discomfort.

"You were great out there, Nia!" The first skater to my right spoke, drawing my attention to them, grinning widely and waiting for my response.

A few others chimed in, thanking me for skating with them, as if I'd gifted them something with simply my presence, which felt absolutely insane.

"No, thanks for letting me skate with you. I think Lonnie's expectations are a little high, and I don't know if I'll be able to keep up with you guys by Saturday." I laughed awkwardly, scratching at the uninjured side of my head. "It was fun skating, though!" I smiled politely, and they all got quiet.

"You're skating Saturday." Harvey's voice came from the far end of the bench, and I watched her stand, skates still on as she took slow strides toward me.

"I would just disappoint you all." I shook my head,

shifting my bag from one shoulder to the other to alleviate the weight of it.

"Disappointment is the only thing we're used to," Harvey said, low enough for only the closest skaters to hear. "What will it take?" she asked.

"What?" I asked.

"What will it take to make it so you don't back out? Skate the bout on Saturday." Her expression was serious; this meant more to her than it did for Lonnie.

Suddenly the weight of disappointing her felt far too heavy for me to carry.

"One condition," I answered with an exhale.

"Name your terms," she said, arms crossed over her chest, looking down at me.

She had a good six inches on me, but with her skates on and mine off, she was easily over six feet tall, making the height difference between us nearly an entire head.

"I need more rink time. I need to build my stamina," I confessed, watching her nod her head at my demands. "I also need skaters," I added hesitantly, watching her eyebrows squeeze together in the middle. "I need a goal to be faster than, so I don't push myself past where I should go. I can't get hurt again."

"That's doable." She nodded, looking over the line of girls on the benches.

"I can help," Mercy volunteered, and then another skater, Beatrix, who went by the name of 'Vominatrix', agreed to donate her time as well.

"Get each other's numbers, make a plan, a schedule, whatever you need to," Harvey directed between the three of us.

"What about you?" I blurted out, honestly surprised she didn't volunteer as well.

Why did I care?

She chuckled. "What about me? Do you need a babysitter?" She tilted her head to the side and gave me that same cocky smirk as the first day she tried to antagonize me into skating with them.

I shrank, finding all my confidence slithering out of my body through my spine, like a tail that would fall off before withering away. "No, it's fine," I said in my quietest voice. She raised a single eyebrow, the look demanding that I confessed, "I'm just... nervous around new people,"

She stared at me blankly, like she wasn't sure what to do with that information.

"It's fine." My mouth worked in rapid fire, my hands waving violently in the air like an apology for even burdening her with my own mental shit.

It was no one else's problem that I'd shut myself in for the last five years, both externally and internally. I lacked practice socially, and it always made me self-conscious, uneasy, constantly second guessing every word and interaction and then torturing myself for hours, even days, following events in an unstoppable cycle of self-analysis and brooding.

I used to be more carefree.

I used to not care.

Maybe it was easier when I was a teenager, or maybe this was just the result of trauma.

I walked past her, saying my goodbyes to the rest of the girls who politely encouraged me to keep skating with them this week. I looked back just as I made my way to the front door, not a single eye on me while they resumed their normal chatter.

They weren't *my* skate family, not the one I had bonded to through blood, sweat, and energy drinks, but there was still a desperate tugging at the very bottom of my soul to belong here too. To be welcomed into the pack. To fit in. To do it all over again, but better, older, wiser this time around. Maybe even stronger.

I wanted to be able to do this without taking my body for granted, to use it as a machine, fine-tuned and cared for through the test of time instead of a weapon, forged with brute demand for strength and sharpness.

I could find the balance between giving my all and giving too much.

We showed up to the rink at seven in the morning the next day, pounding on Lonnie's back door until they came out spitting every curse word under the sun.

"I told you I'd be here early." I shrugged, rubbing my sore thighs from the previous night. All the post-workout supplements in the world weren't going to take away the pain; the only thing I could do was skate through it until it disappeared, though it would likely resurface again tomorrow in double.

I used to thrive there, in that sweet spot where sore muscles were a permanent fixture in my life, because it meant they were always getting stronger. *I was always getting stronger.* Now, not so much. It had taken everything to talk myself out of bed this morning, and the minute I lowered to sit on the toilet, I mentally gave up, swearing that nothing was worth this kind of misery.

And then, she texted me. My phone's volume switch must have flipped at some point, because the notification alert let out that obnoxious, high-pitched ding. It triggered the headache I'd been burying under painkillers for the last two days.

> Got your number from Mercy, be ready in ten.

My heart leaped into my throat. I didn't need to text back asking who it was. I knew. I hadn't even thought twice about the fact that my car was totaled and I had no ride to the rink this morning.

She had, though.

I brushed my teeth and washed my face before taking a good look in the mirror, turning my head to the side to examine the wound for the first time since the accident. Gore wasn't my thing, not since I'd seen my own bones outside my body.

It was drying up, looking like it was scabbing, which was good because the stitches were starting to itch something awful, and my hair was kind of a mess from where Mercy gave me a lazy undercut. I parted it to the opposite side, keeping as much of my hair away from the wound as possible and weaving it in one long braid I threw over my shoulder.

The pink was fading from the ends, the old ombré almost too grown out to be anything but colorful tips. Even the natural brown I'd been cultivating was dull, lackluster, and frizzing at the top. Every part of my hair needed attention, but my life was a set of poorly stacked Jenga blocks, each issue waiting its turn to be carefully pulled out and tended to.

I only took care of a need once it became impossible to ignore.

Only addressed a cavity once it hurt to the point of affecting my appetite, only paid a hospital bill once the collectors began showing up at my door. Only caught up on my utilities once they threatened to turn them off. One at a time, everything eventually got dealt with, even if my life was lived constantly playing catch up.

Always behind.

I pushed the thoughts out of my head once I heard the honk from Harvey's SUV, *The Avett Brothers* blaring way beyond social acceptability for this time in the morning. She grinned the minute I stepped out onto the parking lot, reaching over the passenger side to open the door for me. It was toasty warm, the heat on full blast, and I was thankful for it, rubbing my hands together to thaw out the little bit of chill that had seeped into my bones.

"Do you like *The Arctic Monkeys*?" she yelled over the blasting music instead of turning it down, switching the song.

"It's *Arctic Monkeys,* not *The Arctic Monkeys,*" I corrected her, sticking my tongue out with a teasing that felt familiar.

"The *the* is implied, *trust me.*" She shifted the car in reverse while I laughed.

Then, my mind did that thing where I played back that interaction for the majority of the ride on repeat until I'd found every flaw in the seven words I'd spoken in those fifteen minutes.

Why did I do that? Why did I *always* do that? Always had to say something snarky and sarcastic. Always had a know-it-all response I couldn't hold back, even while dying to make a good impression, to give the illusion of normalcy.

"Hey, uh, my bad," I stumbled through the awkward apology as she slowed into a parking spot.

She stared at me blankly, and when I didn't speak again, she pushed, "For?"

Typical that she hadn't followed along inside my head through the turmoil.

"I don't know, correcting you? The Arctic Monkeys thing? It was so pointless and minimal. I don't know why I felt the need to say it when it obviously doesn't matter. I just don't want you to think I'm some weirdo who just starts correcting people. I promise I don't have to be right all the time." I blurted out, "Okay wait, maybe I do. I don't know. I'm shit at first impressions." I began working through it out loud, a nervous laugh threatening to bubble its way out. "But if I know something to be a fact, my brain just can't sit on the sidelines, no matter how hard I try to hold it back. It physically hurts me."

"It's okay." She smiled, taking the key out of the ignition. "I don't mind being wrong." She reached over my lap, jiggling the inside handle on the passenger's seat until the door came open. "Sorry, the handle gets stuck."

I caught the door before it shut again, both of us grabbing our things and making our way into the gym just to deal with Lonnie's morning rage, which had a lovely aftermath of being forced to skate ten minutes of laps with the same six *ABBA* songs shuffling on repeat while Mo got their coffee mainstreaming into the closest vein. It took three solid attempts at *no* to get the point across that I didn't need coffee to start my day, which was always met with concerned looks.

It was the most Brazilian thing about me, something I'd inherited directly from my mother that made me feel closest to my culture. Coffee wasn't the jumpstart fuel for the day. It wasn't an addiction that needed to be satiated in order to have a good time. It was a social ritual. It was a gathering.

It was part of my culture.

Culture.

A word I'd struggled with for most of my life with a mother who pretended like assimilation had gotten the best of her.

I didn't blame her. It was a survival mechanism, and had she not adapted for survival, she wouldn't have made it in America, the place she thought held every answer to her problems. The fear of being sent back was always too real, so I grew up with whispers in my ear: "Be loud and proud, but don't make too much noise. Be all you can be, but don't let them notice you. Blend in, but be better than the ones before you." An impossible charade to keep up.

With no one to tell me it was okay to just exist as I was, her insecurities leaked onto me, manifesting in ways I couldn't help. I understood Portuguese, but I was too afraid to speak it. I loved the food, knew the recipes, but I had no confidence in cooking them. I only told others I was Brazilian if they asked where my parents were from.

Never where *I* was from, as if obvious by my manner-isms and lack of accent that I was a gringa, something an uncle I'd met once before called me on a trip back to my mother's homeland.

I'd been ignoring her calls for two days now, finding more peace than I had expected and more guilt than I needed. My thoughts always somehow circled back to her, just like any given road in Devil Town could somehow take you back to Skateland.

I thought I needed Harvey as a social crutch so I wouldn't feel so out of place, but Mercy and Beatrix were easy to get along with. Beatrix and I bonded over our shared love for carbon fiber boots, and Mercy was genuinely too sweet for me to find any faults in. I was also still grateful she'd saved me from an emergency room visit, so I owed her every ounce of kindness I could muster.

"I think we'll be able to take those stitches out in a couple days." She rummaged through the hair she'd cut short, examining my healing wound.

"Good; they're driving me insane!" I covered them back up with padded gauze that kept my helmet from rubbing and readied myself for another round of footwork drills.

"Let's grab lunch. I'm famished," Beatrix shouted from across the track, already pulling off her quads and ripping her sweat-drenched tank top off so she could use it to dry her underarms. She tucked the top inside the middle of her sports bra and stood with her hands on her hips as she waited for Mercy and me to exit the track.

"Where's Harvey?" I found the words exiting my mouth before I'd given them too much thought.

Mercy and Beatrix eyed each other for a brief second before Mercy answered, "Probably doing Nadine's bitch work." She snorted a laugh before Beatrix elbowed her in the rib.

"I'd kill for a cheeseburger," I admitted, trying to change the subject from whatever *that* was.

"Ditto. I'll drive," Beatrix volunteered.

We changed into fresh clothes, and I mentally blocked out my own discomfort of knowing my clean clothes were now touching my disgusting, sweat-dried body. The winter weather was still in full force, so a pair of sweatpants and a fluffy fleece sweater under my coat was everything I needed.

Vominatrix drove a Dodge Charger that was likely older than me. It looked to have been yellow once upon a time, but the entire thing was covered in bumper stickers overlapping each other for dominance and attention anywhere glass wasn't present. Right above the right taillight was the one I immediately decided was my favorite, with the words *Honk if you're dead* in neon pink.

I got into the back, not bothering to announce that I couldn't handle it. I decided I'd rather swallow my puke this time around versus telling strangers that if I didn't get the passenger seat, I'd get car sick. Devil Town was small; anywhere we went was likely going to be less than a ten-minute drive.

I could make it.

I did not make it.

Beatrix pulled over into the side of the road, and I sprang the door open, barely sticking my head out in time to spew this morning's electrolytes onto the pavement.

Instantly better, like always.

"Are you sure you're good?" she questioned, suspicion etched on her face, worry for the upholstery of her car likely floating through her head.

"You're not sick, are you?" Mercy's innate medical training kicked in.

"I just get carsick in the back, no biggie. I'm good now." I wiped my mouth with the back of my hand.

"Why didn't you say anything?" Mercy chastised as she unbuckled and dove into the backseat from the passenger side.

"I just don't like to be a bother." I shrugged, knowing my inner turmoil went much deeper than the explanation, but it would suffice.

"Don't be self-sacrificing. I'd rather give up the front seat than smell old puke in Trixie's car for the next six months." She tossed her legs up so her feet could rest on the middle console between me and Beatrix.

Trixie. Cute. The nickname fit her much better than the *Bea* I had made up in my mind. She was about four foot ten, equipped with a blocker's hip that would send fear into any jammer. I certainly didn't want to scrimmage with her on the opposing side; my leg wasn't *that* healed.

During lunch, I found out that Meredith, or Mercy, was driving an hour twice a day, four days a week, to come out here for practices, since she worked at the children's hospital two counties over. She still lived with her mom, and with all her expenses from school, it made more sense to make the commute then it did to pay rent somewhere else.

Trixie, who ate a veggie burger not because she was a vegetarian but because she didn't trust other people to cook her meat, was the newest member to the team, having moved to Devil Town about eight months prior for a teaching job at the high school. She was married to a data analyst who worked from home and watched their fifteen-month-old baby.

So normal.

Not a mental illness in sight.

I had to be careful; I had an awful tendency of turning any stable, nurturing energy around me into a mother-figure, and it was a surefire way to ruin the prospect of a friendship.

Then again, I was thinking long term when I only had four or so days left until the bout, maybe five until I'd get on that plane and never look back. Chewing my burger and nodding as the girls dished out important background information about their fellow teammates, I made a mental note to text Lonnie to check that they in fact already *had* gotten me my ticket home.

Home.

Wherever that was. An empty New York apartment far away from here.

During lunch, I also found out I forgot to turn off an auto-pay bill I was definitely planning on letting slide into collection, and now the rest of my planned savings for this trip had dwindled down to the last six dollars and thirty two cents in my account.

For the rest of the week.

I didn't want to think about it.

My mother must have been doing some form of witch-craft to make sure I'd need to call her, to depend on her.

I refused.

I pulled my phone out and sent the inquiry to Lonnie.

> Negative, ghost rider. I'll purchase the flight when you fulfill your end of the bargain.

> Lonnie, the flight will be sold out!

> O no. *tears*

Putting my phone away, I tried to hide any visible signs of my frustration and blocked Lonnie from my thoughts so their decisions wouldn't sour my day. All of this had been on purpose. They knew there would be no plane tickets left, knew it meant I'd have to stay here longer, that I'd inevitably skate with the Dames until I destroyed all my plans in exchange for this life again.

I pushed down the spiteful part of me that wanted to do the opposite. These skaters deserved better than that, better than both what Lonnie or I could offer.

"You really are fast!" Mercy shouted from behind me over the sounds of our skates against the track.

I let my laughter trail back with my braid, blowing and whipping against my neck. I didn't have a trick to it, and it definitely wasn't that I was in better shape than any of them. It was just easy for me. My brain knew I needed to just be faster than *them* and with my legs in charge, my body made it happen.

My laughter quieted with the sound of the double doors slamming against the wall behind them as Harvey burst in, looking angry as hell, half her gear already on and her helmet under her right arm. The pissed off look on her face was doubly amplified by her quick strides.

Tossing her gym bag on the bench, skates in hand, she made her way to the locker rooms without gazing our way. I caught another knowing look from Mercy to Trixie that seemed less gossip and more concern this time around.

"Is she okay?" I immediately regretted prying.

I was no one to these people. How dare I wedge myself in and demand they lay their feelings and problems out in front of me?

"Don't ask," they both answered in perfect sync before they looked at each other and burst out laughing. "She'll be fine once she skates it off," Mercy assured.

And she did. After two or three laps, whatever temper had come in with her had dissipated with another friendly match, where this time, I very clearly kicked her ass. We both laid on the track, chests heaving after fifteen laps. Neither of us spoke for minutes until finally, Harvey flipped on her stomach and crawled toward me.

How she had the energy for it after that was beyond me.

"You'll need to pass your skills test before the bout," she reminded me, raising a concerned eyebrow. "You think you can do it?"

"Well, if I can't, then it looks like you better get faster." I chuckled.

"Your corners are tight. It's impossible to pass you when you get to the turn first," she said with an admiration that hit me exactly where it needed to, melting away some of my insecurities.

"It *is* possible," I told her, remembering that all it took was someone with enough force to knock my brain around my skull to get me out of one of those tight corners.

"You just need more core training. Once your center of gravity is low and solid, even Trix can't knock you down," she assured, as if she had all the faith in me.

"You say that like I'm looking to go back into skating permanently." I shook my head before propping myself up onto my elbows.

"You can keep lying to yourself all you want, princess, but it's pretty obvious you want to be here." She stood, an air of annoyance returning to her.

Was she mad? At *me*?

"I never said I didn't want to be here. There's nowhere on this planet I love more than Skateland, but staying isn't logical, nor is it part of my plans. I've spent every moment of my life skipping from one impulsive decision to the next, and for once in my life, I have a plan," I told her, knowing I didn't owe her an explanation, but feeling the weight of needing to get the words out. "I just need to get this one thing right," I whispered.

"And then what?" she asked, the annoyance fading again.

"I don't know." I shook my head honestly.

"Take your skills test on Friday. That gives you two more full days to skate and get your stamina up." She danced back to our previous conversation.

"Feels impossible," I confessed.

"You're already better than you were yesterday. You can do this." She smiled, that same cocky smile as always, but with her faith directed at me, it was damn good encouragement.

There were only two mandatory practices a week, and it didn't look like other teams were using Skateland anymore for their scrimmages. Lonnie still kept the place open for whoever wanted to practice, and because the Dames were hungry for a win, most of them showed up five days a week.

By the time the rest of the squad had made their way to the rink for practice, I was ready to throw in the towel again. My muscles were beyond angry, on a level of sore I hadn't known in years. My feet were scorching hot below me, aching for a break, and my toenails dug into the fabric of my skates even through thick socks.

"I don't think I can do another hour," I confessed as almost every skater from the previous night aside from Nadine filed their way onto the track.

"Only thirty since you can't scrimmage yet." Harvey grinned, like she was giving me a silver lining.

"If I skate for thirty more minutes, I'm gonna need to be carried out of here," I warned, no bravado left, the need to prove myself no longer existing in my bones.

"That can be arranged." She laughed, pushing me toward the incoming pack.

"I'm not kidding. I'll be useless tomorrow, I'm gonna be so sore," I shouted back to her as we merged with the rest of the skaters, lapping around the track for their warmups.

"You'll be fine. Harvey gives good leg rubs." Trixie gave me the softest hip bump she was capable of before falling back and chatting with another skater.

That sounded amazing. I hadn't had a massage since I'd deviated from my degree that one semester and burned some credits taking a *crystal healing* class and *introduction to massage*. I'd only done it because I heard the students practiced on each other, and I couldn't afford physical therapy for my leg anymore.

It was a resourceful solution, but it extended my time in undergrad by an entire year, and since I had postponed college for roller derby, it made me a twenty-seven-year-old graduate. Not my mother's proudest moment, considering she'd been the first in her family to not only graduate, but obtain multiple doctorates.

Everyone has their time. Their seasons, my grandmother would tell me any time she felt her daughter's pressure weighing me down. She was my beacon of hope, the positive voice in my head that told me I could do anything.

But then she died, and so did that little voice, leaving me with only my mother's judgements and doubts to fill my brain. It'd been too long since I felt her encouragement, her warmth. I could barely remember her voice anymore. What I would give to hear it, to give her a little sniff, a cheirinho.

I shook the thought away and moved my legs faster once I realized I was being left behind by the pack. A skater in bright green pigtails fell in with me, the ninety-six on her arm indicative of a birth year.

"I'm really glad you're here!" she yelled over the collective noise, not waiting for me to respond. "It means your mother was right all along." Goosebumps covered my body as her smile faded.

"What?" I asked. Had I misheard her?

"I said," she yelled louder, "it means Lonnie was right all along. They always said you'd eventually come home."

I looked over at her, lingering on her features and digging through the memories of dozens of yearbook photos. That long green hair was once brown and kept short, and the tattoo of a barbed wire heart on her throat certainly wasn't there in high school.

"Ash!" I blurted out. "When did you start skating?"

Ashlee James was a year younger than me, and we ended up taking some art electives together my junior and senior year. I hadn't talked to her again after grade school. I assumed she'd gone to college somewhere while I stayed behind skating, but here she was, the name *Fearleader* across the back of her practice shirt and a pair of skates that looked more broken in than my own.

"Not long after you left. I had just moved back to Devil Town when they televised that bout." She tried not to emphasize the *that,* but she didn't need to. We both knew which bout she was referring to.

Catching up with Ash made it easy to forget the burn in my legs and skate the rest of warmups without dreading every single minute. It felt good to have a familiar face to count on, something that didn't make me feel so much like a stranger in my own hometown.

But at almost twenty-eight, that was the only thing I could be. Everyone in my age group had moved on, and those who hadn't, I likely didn't tolerate then and wouldn't be tolerating now. I looked around the track, really looked at every single skater's face, and realized that I didn't recognize any of them at all.

Not that I had expected to, but the realization was alarmingly lonely.

Mo blew the whistle. "Ladders!" they yelled, and every one of us moved into two lines, assembling for footwork drills. "Not you, Nia. Lonnie says you're doing speed and skills test tonight."

"What?" came out of my mouth simultaneously with Harvey, who was already in line for ladders.

"I thought I'd test Friday? Get more time to practice." The panic grew too quickly for me to attempt to hide or mask it. Being tested too soon could have devastatingly mortifying consequences to my ego, the kind I wasn't ready to mentally face yet.

"It's way too soon." Harvey came to my defense, skating out of the queue.

"No-go, Buckaroos. Lonnie wants a scrimmage under your belt before the game, so we gotta get you passing your skills ASAP," Mo explained.

"What if I don't pass?" I said as quietly as possible, hoping no other skater could hear my lack of confidence.

"Then you test again tomorrow, and the next day. Until Saturday, I guess." They laughed, not seeming to care how long it would take me to skate my twenty-seven laps in the required time.

"Where's Lonnie?" I asked.

"Visiting their mom in hospice. Pick two skaters to skate with you." They grabbed a timer from their pocket and lifted the neckband over their head to hang it down their chest.

I commanded my stomach to chill and at least wait until I'd skated before the vomit-fest and-slash-or shit-fest started. Asking two skaters to pass a speed test with me was social torture. No one alive wanted to be forced to speed-skate twenty-seven laps more than the necessary amount of times, not to mention risk the ever-looming embarrassment of not making it and being ridiculed by your teammates.

I couldn't volunteer someone else into that.

I didn't dare catch Harvey's gaze. Looking at Mo, I shook my head, the panicked expression on my face enough to tell them I'd rather skate it alone than force someone into it unwillingly.

"Suit yourself. Get in position." They whistled again, and my stomach dropped.

Every skater in the middle of footwork drills paused to

turn in my direction. I swallowed the hardest lump my throat had ever amassed. They would all be watching me, the entire time.

I skated over to my cubby, taking a small sip of water to quench my thirst. I wanted to drown in it, to chug the entire bottle, but there was nothing worse than the feeling of skating with water sloshing around in my belly. Wiping the dripping water from my chin, I rolled my shoulders back and took my place.

A few nervous jiggles got all my nerves out before I signaled to Mo that I was ready.

Was I ready?

Shit.

Here went... literally nothing.

The whistle blew.

The trick was to not burn out too fast. I couldn't use all my energy in the beginning trying to go turbo mode. Pacing was important, even for the fastest of skaters. It was almost smarter to reserve my energy for the end, for the necessary boost to keep me going once I'd inevitably tire.

Mo would be judging every minute, and the worst part was, I had no idea if I had the standard WFTDA–Women's Flat Track Roller Derby– five minutes, or only four of them. They'd be timing every lap, examining every crossover, scrutinizing the depth of my squat, and when I was done, they'd judge the way I stopped. All of it was necessary to make sure a skater was ready for bouting.

But was *I* ready for bouting?

I had lost count of laps around sixteen. I could hear the drone of skaters surrounding the flat-track, counting each time I went over the finish line, cheering bloody murder for me with every lap I pushed through. I couldn't remember a time I'd worked harder for anything in my life. Even my previous speed tests had never taken so much out of me. With them, I had weeks, months, of training under my belt.

This felt impossible, but I'd never needed anything more.

I wanted this with my entire body and soul.

I fought off the cramps in my stomach. One after the other, my legs moved, disconnected from my brain and the pain radiating through my calves and my thighs. I thought I heard twenty, but there was a good chance I had also heard Mo say I wasn't going to make it.

I only let the defeat burn through me for a few seconds, determined to not give up, determined to be good enough. Every pass of my feet became heavier, every rub of my thighs through netted stockings chafing harder, making each crossover more unbearable than the last.

Then Mad Mo blew that damn whistle again.

Sliding into a hockey stop on the sides of my wheels, I froze, halfway around the track while swallowing the bile that journeyed up my throat. The finish line was at least fifteen feet away. I didn't have to look at a single face to know I hadn't done it. I hadn't met the minimum requirement. A mortifying rage dug its claws into me, and all I could focus on was the need to bolt.

To escape.

My lungs were scorching, but every part of my body refused to react, refused to break, until I could do it in private.

I knew I wasn't ready.

I knew it.

My brain blocked out any sound, though I wasn't sure there were any noises in the entire rink aside from my skates gliding over the wooden track. My entire body was worn down, aching. Eventually, my feet took me to the locker room, where I spilled my body carelessly over a wooden bench and shattered.

There was no way to discern if the tears were from the disappointment of my own failure, or an organic response to my exhaustion, my body telling me to stop and lay down for a week or two after the spontaneous burst of exercise. It was impossible to dissect the physical from the mental.

A light knock sounded against the locker room door.

I didn't respond. It wasn't locked, and I had no authority to keep anyone out. Maybe they weren't even here for me.

The knock came again.

"Nia?"

My self-loathing rose to a maximum, shreds of my dignity flaking off me like dry skin in the winter. I wanted to disappear. I *needed* to disappear. Fatigue had my entire body trembling, droplets of sweat still hanging from my fingertips, waiting for their turn to fall.

The worst part was admitting that this had meant so much to me.

It had meant *too* much.

"I've given you the standard two-minute lonely pity-party, and that's about as long as I can hold them back for," Harvey warned from outside, and within seconds, Vomina-trix and Mercy were filing inside the locker room with a few other skaters who had been friendly with me.

They gave their condolences gleefully, as if they couldn't feel the shame practically evaporating out of my pores like salt ridden sweat. I couldn't form words, only nodding and smiling politely to avoid embarrassing myself further.

Before I'd even had time to sit myself up on the bench, the entire squad was packed into the locker room. It reminded me of the year a tornado hit during practice, and we all crammed in here for three hours while listening to the branches fall on the roof. It took an entire week to clean the debris, but the insurance payout was enough for us to make some upgrades to the rink.

Lonnie had called it a win-win, but it took them months to stop sleeping with a sound machine to drown out any possible storms in the middle of the night. At the time, it hadn't felt like this big, scary thing that was happening. Lonnie had distracted us, quizzing us on derby stats and making up games to pass the time.

Nobody had been there to distract Lonnie, though.

I snapped back to the presently overstuffed locker room, the smell of sweaty protective gear becoming too over-whelming to ignore. I hadn't looked up, hadn't made eye contact with a single one of them yet.

Burning with social discomfort and unable to run anywhere, I hid behind my own hands, covering up the evidence of my tears as best as possible.

"Well, looks like Nadine's is off the roster for a hang-out spot tonight. Where are we going?" the one with *Rae-volver* on the back of her shirt asked with a snort.

She was promptly elbowed in the side by a girl I hadn't met yet and then given matching dirty looks by at least three other skaters I could count.

"She's just going through some... growing pains," the curly-haired girl whose name I'd learned was *Jackie the Rip-*

her assured, giving Harvey an awkward stare. "Pony up, babe."

The skaters all joined together, a drone of collaborative efforts to convince Harvey to donate her place for a party.

She sighed, like they were all too exhausting to argue or fight with. "We can chill at my place, but if you guys harass my neighbor again, I'm going to have to move."

A wild cheer erupted from the group. Almost as quickly as they had come in, they changed out of their sweaty clothes and filed out, leaving me in the locker room.

Except for Harvey, who hadn't moved an inch from where she stood over me, arms crossed over her chest.

"You good?" she asked.

I didn't look up. What was I even supposed to say? The socially acceptable lie that would remove any burden or obligation from the kind stranger in front of me to stay behind and make me feel better? Or the truth that felt quite literally like hot magma at my throat, scorching to free itself, though I knew from conditioning that it should be held back?

"I don't know," I offered something in between.

"Come hang out." She didn't so much ask so much as she told me.

"I don't know." I repeated, shaking my head.

"Is it us?" she asked.

I shook my head once more.

It *was* them, though. They were too much. Too nice, too good, too familiar, and it made me feel things I wasn't prepared to feel.

No, that was a lie too.

"It's me," I admitted.

"Then come hang out. If the problem is you, then you, I can deal with." She stuck her hand out in offering. "We can talk about it, or not mention it at all tonight, or ever again. It's up to you."

There was something reassuring about her promise and the ease that came with it made me feel lighter.

I sighed, nodding as I took her hand and stood.

Harvey had a one-bedroom apartment just minutes from Skateland. Aside from Nadine, she was apparently one of the only other skaters on the team who had their own place. A few of them didn't even live in town, and the idea that they were commuting to skate was a commitment I couldn't hide being impressed by.

I rode with Harvey, but the other skaters had already gotten there by the time we arrived. Waiting for her had been deemed unnecessary, as apparently someone knew which rock the spare key was kept under.

"What do you do?" I asked, filling up the awkward space so as not to be burdened by my own overly critical thoughts.

"Graphic design. I mostly work from home," she explained as we walked from the car to her door.

"You moved here just to do graphic design from home?" I laughed, wondering if I'd lock myself in a place like this if I had the freedom to go anywhere.

"How do you know I didn't grow up here?" she asked, a playful curiosity on her face.

"I'm assuming we're about the same age, I don't remember you from school." *Dear Lord, please kill me if I'm wrong. I am not strong enough to face the mortifying embarrassment of admitting I may have ignored this girl for years in school.*

"I'm twenty-six, and yeah, moving to Devil Town probably sounds like a downgrade, unless you're coming from Smithville." She chuckled.

"Oh my God! You grew up in Smithville?" I made a fake gagging noise after the town's name. "You couldn't pay me to drive through it anymore. I've spent so much money on speeding tickets there." Smithville was a podunk little four-street town on the edge of our city, and while *we* thought we were tiny, Smithville was miniscule in comparison.

"That's all we have over there. Speed traps and churches," she admitted with a nod.

Even with its less than ten thousand population, Smithville still had its own education system and was considered too far outside Devil Town city limits for its youth to attend our schools. The chance we would have met back then was rare.

She didn't bother with the key, the noise coming from the door was all she needed to push it open and reveal the party inside. It was a cute little place, a newer complex I didn't remember from my time before, and by the look of the updated floors and cabinets, it was definitely a newer build.

There was a loud cheer from the skaters once we came through. A smile I couldn't hide spread over my face at feeling welcomed, and I decided I'd try not to get hung up on the devastating failure that loomed over me. I wouldn't let it continue to suffocate all happiness from my life. At least for tonight.

I was just passing through. It didn't even matter anyway. Right?

"I'm wrecked," I admitted, practically slithering my way through the circle of girls shotgunning cans of alcoholic seltzer in Harvey's kitchen, dumping my body on the empty couch.

As if my corpse had a sensor, letting it know the last two days were coming to an end and that it could finally stop playing at being strong, everything began to ache all at once.

"You look dead," Mercy laughed, handing me a beer.

"I feel it," I admitted, reaching for the can but searching for Harvey, finding her leaning against her kitchen counter with a soda in her hand.

I remembered what she said about Lonnie kicking her off the team if she couldn't bout sober.

"I'm good." I waved the beer away. "I'll be even more sore if I drink tonight. Everything hurts," I whined.

It didn't feel fair, didn't feel right to drink. Here she was, letting everyone use her home, letting them drink in her space, when it was probably itching at her very soul to do the same.

"It's not that deep," Harvey's voice came from behind the couch. "You can drink with them. I'm a big girl."

Goosebumps prickled at the back of my neck. How she had gotten behind me so fast, I wasn't sure, but there was something about the way I always looked for her and how she always appeared that was far too comforting, far too easy to rely on.

I hadn't had anyone I could count on in too long to remember.

"If I drink, I'll be too sore to skate the rest of the week," I explained. Though it wasn't the real reason, it was *a* truth, and for now, it would be enough.

Within seconds, she was standing by the couch again, this time with a can of sparkling water in her other hand, offering it to me. Grateful, I barely lifted my shoulders off the couch, reaching forward with one hand to take it.

"So you *are* skating again this week?" She lifted my feet, just high enough so she could sit on the couch herself.

When I moved to give her space, her grip on my ankles tightened, holding my feet over her lap. Nobody else seemed to be interested in sitting, so I didn't bother, quieting the part of my brain that kept telling me I was the rudest person in existence for taking up so much space.

"I don't know," I finally answered after some time, toying with the tab on the can before popping it open. "Not sure I can mentally handle failing a second time." I focused on the can and nothing else in the room, my vision blurring just slightly as I worked my hardest to avoid her stare.

"That's a shame. Would have been killer to skate with you." She shrugged, taking a large gulp of her soda.

"Yeah, sure." I scoffed. "I can't even skate twenty-seven in five. What makes you think I would have done anything helpful in a bout?" I challenged, the cynicism working its way out of me again.

"I had to take my skills test four times," she admitted, raising both eyebrows high up her forehead as she waited for my reaction.

I had none. She was bullshitting me, just trying to make me feel better.

"Angelina Roll-ie," she yelled from the couch.

"What's up?" a shout came from the other side of the room.

"How many times did you take your skills test?" she asked.

"Are we counting the times we had to call paramedics?" Angelina yelled again, the question making me spit some of my water out.

"You know we don't count medical for tap outs!" Harvey shouted back.

"At least five!" Angelina Roll-ie responded proudly, and the skaters all cheered.

"Vominatrix!" Harvey called to the crowded room.

"Twice," she chirped cheerfully from the corner, understanding the assignment.

Harvey continued, yelling out a few more names until she'd successfully proven her point. None of them had passed their skills test the first time, and with five years in a capsule, frozen in time, my skates buried under a pile of nostalgia in a storage locker waiting for death or rebirth, I somehow expected to be better?

To be faster and stronger on my second day than these skaters who were giving it their all four to five days a week?

I was officially stuck, a prisoner between two feelings, wanting nothing more than to claim this life again, to cement my quads to my feet and be Nia-Death-Experience once more. To be given the chance to do it over and do it right this time.

The other feeling involved throwing my gear in the

trash for good, hitchhiking to New York, and never looking back. Because underneath all the desire, all the drive, all the thrill, I knew I risked hurting myself all over again by just skating on that track. There was no coming back from another injury.

Not whole.

"What are you afraid of?" Harvey asked when I said nothing more.

"All of it. Success, failure, everything in between." I shrugged, my confession catching her off guard and forcing a reflexed squeeze from her hands still wrapped around my shins. I groaned, the tenderness in my muscles already set in. "I think you owe me a leg rub."

She laughed, pushing the hair from her green eyes before she squeezed again. "I don't remember offering."

"I'm pretty sure Trixie volunteered you," I reminded her.

"If you're afraid of failing *and* succeeding, then what are you left with?" She resumed the conversation like it had never been interrupted, her thumbs digging into the muscles of my calves, using just the right amount of pressure that teetered between relief and pain.

Walking was going to be a struggle tomorrow.

"I don't know." I closed my eyes, allowing myself to enjoy this brief moment of comfort as her fingers moved diligently. "Limbo, I guess."

"Limbo isn't meant to be permanent," she said softly, continuing to work through the angry muscles.

"It's easier than moving on." I was melting into the furniture, uncaring that there was an actual party happening around us, becoming one with the couch while

Harvey soothed the ache in my legs. "That's nice," I breathed out, setting the can on the floor next to me.

"How's your head?" she asked. I didn't bother opening my eyes.

"I barely feel it now." It was the truth, aside from the occasional beeping in the back of my mind. I chalked it up to just another one of the random sounds my brain could pick up on and decided it was likely part of my new normal after the accident. No need to get it checked out.

Not until it became intolerable.

I couldn't focus on the next thing she said. The day caught up to me, and the room had suddenly quieted. I was too tired to care, too comfortable to want to.

T here was nothing better than waking up from satisfied sleep, the kind that wasn't followed by any obligations, no alarm set. The type of rest reserved for children, that wasn't appreciated until it was too far out of reach. I patted around blindly for my phone to check the time, giving up once I felt it somewhere near my head. It was long dead, the battery drained between the ride from Skateland to Harvey's apartment, but I hadn't bothered to charge it during the night.

I finally opened my eyes to the room around me. It had to be nearly noon, but every curtain was closed, every blind drawn tight. I scratched the sleep away from my eyes, stretching my legs to find my feet still very much on Harvey's lap, who slept sitting up, head tilted back, resting on the couch.

I poked the side of her leg with my big toe. On the third poke her lip curled up into a smile. "Mmm?" she grumbled.

"You can't be comfortable," I whispered, looking around

to make sure I wasn't going to be waking anyone who might be passed out in a corner.

But there was no one here. The apartment was completely empty, spotless, actually, as if no one had been here at all last night. No cans lay around, no dirty cups, no sign of pizza boxes, and if I sniffed hard enough, there was a slight hint of citrus in the air.

Had somebody cleaned?

"Best sleep of my life," she mumbled. "What time is it?"

"No clue; my phone is dead," I told her, prolonging the inevitable feeling of the real world bombarding me once I turned it back on.

Stretching her arms overhead in an exaggerated stretch, she yawned, her legs sticking out from the couch before she shook it off and turned to me.

"So?" There was no need for a pause or for further questions; I knew where those two letters were headed.

"I'm not ready to talk about it," I admitted, shaking my head. "But I'm not sure I'm ready to quit either."

She smirked. "Take the day off from skating," she suggested. "Try again tomorrow."

"And do what?" I laughed. "There's nothing for me to do in Devil Town if I'm not skating."

"What's waiting for you where you're going?" she asked.

A loaded question.

"An entry level job that will pay for an apartment the size of a utility closet." I shrugged, hesitating before finishing, "My mother."

Her eyes perked up. "Oh. Are you close?"

"We're a lot of things. Lacking boundaries, mutually

emotionally manipulative, codependent, damaged as hell, but close?" I shook my head. "Surprisingly, I don't think my mother knows a single thing about me that actually matters," I admitted out loud for the first time in my life.

"That's rough," she said, moving my legs to the side and standing up. "Mother wounds are lethal."

Mother wound.

Mine wasn't a wound—it was a festering sore. It blistered and pussed, stretching the skin until it was ready to burst. It threatened to seep into my family tree the minute I gave birth someday.

Cyclical.

"You have no idea," I told her, standing and groaning at the pull on my tight muscles.

"That bad?" she chuckled.

"Probably worse had you not rubbed the crap out of them last night." I pressed out the wrinkles on my sweats, knowing it did nothing except soothe a nervous need.

"Pass your skills tomorrow, and I'll rub them every night until you leave." She tossed the words over her shoulder as she disappeared into the hallway.

"That's a deal." I jumped at the offer, "Don't mess with me. I'm worse than a debt collector!" I promised, her laugh echoing from the open door.

"I need to shower. Do you need coffee?" she yelled from the room.

"No, I'm good," I responded, finally grabbing my phone from the crevice of the couch where I'd stuck it for good measure, finding a rogue charger near the closest outlet to plug into.

It always took way too long to come back to life, as if the

sweet release of death was somehow more comforting than working its little robotic battery to be a servant for the human race. It was usually time to talk it out again in therapy when I started to feel empathy towards my inanimate objects.

"Antônia, your teddy bears aren't jealous of each other. You don't need to keep them all on your bed. You're not getting enough sleep at night," my mother would tell me as a child. *"I promise, your notebooks aren't sad because you've gotten a new one,"* she'd assure me as I cried over the pile of untouched notepads.

It never worked.

My brain was the captain of the ship, but the waters were dark and murky. I could find empathy for a chipping patch of paint if I tried.

My phone turned on, and the first text was from Mercy, saying she wanted to take my stitches out either today or tomorrow. Then came the flood of missed calls, video chat attempts, and voicemails from my mother, every hour on the hour, even in the middle of the night. I opened the texts, reading the most recent one first.

> I will not lose my daughter.

And she said *I* was the one constantly catastrophizing.

The phone vibrated in my hand, the incoming call too predictable for me to be surprised in any way, but the visceral reaction was still a biological conditioning. My heart raced, my hands clammy as I ground my teeth, clenching them tighter than reasonable. It was easy for her to make me feel like a fifteen-year-old again, constantly policed by a parent who couldn't trust me to make a single decision on my own, so I lied and hid whatever I could any chance I got.

Sure, maybe if I had been capable of making any safe or sound decisions for myself, she wouldn't have had to, but all I wanted was room to grow, room to fuck up, to explode and implode, and be able to come back to myself again without the cruel scorn of judgement.

"You'll understand when you become a parent."

"So if I don't want to curse a child with the burden of our generational trauma, I'll never understand you?" Words I'd never be brave enough to tell her.

I held the phone in my hand, shaking as the tears fell silently over the cracked screen until her name disappeared. It came on again, relentless to berate me and tell me I was no good at being in charge of my own life. That I wasn't a capable adult.

That I still needed her.

And here I was, proving her right.

"Are you okay?" Harvey stood at the threshold of the hallway, a sports bra on and baggy jeans hanging from her hips, the buttons not yet clasped and a pair of boxers peeking out from the top. She scuffled her hair in a towel, drying it as much as possible before dropping it to the ground and fingering through the longer, still wet strands in the front.

I didn't think I had ever stared at another girl's face so much in my life.

Though I wasn't measuring past times.

I often spent my class periods distracted, staring off into the face of any girl whose features were the exact opposite of mine. I wanted to be like them, to look like them, to look like anyone who didn't resemble me. I wanted to be them.

Maybe I wanted to be her too.

Strong enough to be a blocker, to handle a hit without shattering. Fast enough to keep up in a jam. Could never be me. Not me and my weak frame.

Ossinho de Sabiá. Bird-boned, like my grandmother would say about me.

Fragile.

I had worked hard to get my legs strong back then, but now, five years later, it was like they'd never been there at all, atrophied from time and fatigue.

Harvey's shadow cast over me, her toes an inch away from mine, the image of them fuzzy through tear filled eyes. She squatted, and I lifted my gaze to meet hers. Tilting her head sideways in silent confusion, she lowered her eyes to my phone, where the word *Mãe* flashed on repeat with another incoming call.

"You don't want to answer?" she asked with a wince, like she was afraid of prying.

"I'm not ready. Don't even know what I would say." I shrugged.

"You're Brazilian?" The line between her eyebrows creased.

"How can you tell?" I fought a chuckle; maybe it was obvious by my blatant fear of my own mother.

"I know a couple words. Mãe is mother, right?" she asked.

I nodded, wiping the newest tears that threatened to fall before they'd gotten a chance.

"Is it going to kill her if you don't answer right now?" she checked, and I shook my head. "Is it going to kill *you?*"

I took a deep breath, shaking my head again with the exhale.

"Then answer when you're ready." She made it sound so easy.

"You don't know Gloria Da Silva. She'll call a SWAT team eventually if I worry her enough." A dry laugh escaped me. "I ran away from home at seventeen once, and she convinced the police to track me down." The memory was so clear, it felt like no time had passed since I had been that teenager, packing a bag after a fight and scurrying off to shack up with a drug dealer who could soothe whatever impulsive itch needed scratched next.

It took her two weeks to find me.

"I will not lose my daughter." She spoke the familiar words that very same day as she hugged me, pulling me from the back of a police car.

As much as I hated it, as much as I hated her, there was no amputating the limb from the body. For every day I had felt a prisoner of my mother's plans, of her expectations was also another day she had saved me. The tight lock of her culture's embrace refused to let me go, refused to abandon me to my own devices, no matter how poor my choices were.

I knew because I had more dead friends who didn't make it past twenty than I had surviving ones I could still call.

"Well, that sounds like a tomorrow problem. And you know what we say to those?" Harvey asked, and I shook my head. "Not today."

I laughed, probably harder than I needed to, but it was too wholesome and dorky not to release some of the heaviness weighing me down. I wiped the remaining trail of tears from my cheek, inhaling a stuttered breath with my next words.

"You were angry before practice last night," I said, weighing the possibility I was overstepping, but hoping that if I could answer a question about my mom, then this wouldn't be too personal to share. Suddenly it wasn't about deflecting the conversation from me. I wanted to know about her, share our problems. "If you don't want to tell me, it's fine," I added, immediately tucking my tail between my legs.

"My own fault," she assured me. "I have this problem where I keep letting people take from me, even when I have nothing left to give."

There it was: the thing that made her tick. The root of it all. I could practically hear my mother salivating from across state lines at the prospect of analyzing her. As for me? I saw it clearly from the very minute we met. It was apparent in every action, every gesture, that Harvey was someone who had been constantly pouring from an empty cup, hoping it would somehow find its way full again.

Was there anyone pouring back into her?

I took the response for what it was and decided to move on, not wanting to intrude or prod and possibly push away the closest thing I'd made to a friend since I'd left this city.

"So...what are we doing?" I asked instead.

"We?" She raised an eyebrow.

My stomach sank.

I am the president of the I-hate-Antônia-club. I'm also the V.P, the secretary, and the treasurer.

"I...uh," I stammered, stumbling over every vowel and syllable that came out of the intolerable waste-hole that was my mouth. "I just assumed when you said take the day off..." I stopped, too embarrassed to admit I'd mistaken a suggestion to distract myself as an invitation.

"If you wanna hang out, we can hang out." She laughed. "I can play hooky at work today, no big deal." She grinned like it was nothing.

"Are you sure?" I hesitated, not wanting to make myself any more of a burden.

"No one will miss me. I think an off day will do us both good." She straightened her legs, standing from her squat and extending a hand to help me do the same. "Come on, I'll take you out for lunch."

"Great, I'm starving." My stomach rumbled, reminding me I hadn't eaten since lunch the previous day. "Can we stop at the motel so I can shower and change?"

"Yup," she said, swiping her keys off the counter and gesturing toward the door.

"Are you sure you don't mind?" I doubled back, remembering what she'd just said about pouring from an empty cup.

"It's just a ride, Nia." She shook her head in disbelief, hiding a smile while she chewed at the dry, cracked bits of her lower lip.

"You've helped me a lot..." I said sincerely as we walked through the doors and faced the winter air. "I don't want to take advantage of your overly helpful nature."

"Well, I'm not that generous," she warned. "I *do* have ulterior motives, remember?" She threw a crooked smirk my way as she entered the car, reaching over to open the door from inside to let me in.

"Your ulterior motives involve getting me to heal from the complex trauma of an injury that's haunted me for five years. Somehow, I'm not sure even the most selfish reason would categorize you as a red flag here," I pointed out sarcastically as I buckled in.

She shrugged. "I guess we'll find out."

CHAPTER 12
EXPULSION

Returning to the motel for the first time in twenty-four hours was an odd feeling. It was supposed to be my landing pad, a place to come home to, even though I had no home. I'd been floating for the last five years, dorm rooms and shared college housing with strangers I'd never bothered to get to know.

What was the point? College was temporary, and I couldn't handle the thought of developing attachments to more people I would just someday leave. So, I kept my head down, did my assignments, and passed my exams. My only lifeline or social contact had been my mother's daily phone calls and a girl named Julie who had been too oblivious to feel rejected by my cold responses. I'd learned her last name just in time for her to graduate, leaving me behind for my extra year of catch-up.

The thought of Julie made me want to reach for my phone, to see if I still had the few texts she'd sent me, even though I never saved her number. I considered sending a message wishing her well, let her know that she had crossed my mind, but it had been a year since she graduated, and I'd come to realize that most people didn't have the same 'out of sight, out of mind' way of thinking when it came to tangible people in their lives.

People weren't forgotten just because they weren't present.

My mother had somehow managed to become the only relationship I could put enough effort into to maintain long distance. The effort in question was answering a phone call, something I seemed to be struggling to do since I'd crashed back into Devil Town.

"She's calling again?" Harvey asked, catching me in a paralyzed trance, watching my phone vibrate in my hands.

I nodded, letting out an exhaustive sigh as I pocketed my phone and slid the keycard over the lock. I dropped my gear bag to the floor within three seconds of making it inside the hotel room, but before I'd even trekked over to my bed, Harvey had already picked it up behind me and placed it on one of the luggage racks meant for the very purpose.

"Where are we going?" I asked, rummaging through my suitcase, trying to find something that would be equally warm and comfortable. This time of the year required multitudes of layers, which was a sensory experience I couldn't fully get behind.

The only layers that were Nia-approved were usually a pair of fishnets under my skating shorts. Anything else was borderline seventh circle of Hell torture. I wasn't meant for cold weather; genetically, I was Brazilian–Baiana to be more precise—and my body craved warmth, sweat, nearly intolerable heat. Hell could also be described as the feeling of multiple layers of fabric in the folds of my knees and elbows.

"Let's get tapas," she chirped, knocking her shoes off her feet and dropping down on the queen-sized bed with her hands behind her head.

"Sounds good," I nodded, grabbing my toiletry bag and heading for the bathroom. "There's drinks in the fridge if you're thirsty."

The door was undamaged, like someone had replaced it since the last time I had been here when Harvey had been forced to break through it. I felt uneasy at the thought of maintenance being in my room, but it was the question of how much this new door was going to cost me that was pressing at the back of my mind.

I removed my sweats, turning the hot water on full blast, wishing this motel had a bathtub. I was grateful for the kitchenette, but there was something about soaking in a hot tub that made all my problems disappear momentarily. Pain, anxiety, sickness—a hot bath cured it every time.

I settled for the shower, sitting on the ground and letting it pour over me. I'd have to deal with my mother eventually. I knew that. But I also knew I was exactly where Harvey had said I was, stuck in limbo. Until I knew exactly what I wanted from my life, I wouldn't be able to leave Devil Town. It was clear my unresolved business here would follow me for the rest of my life.

I needed closure, whatever that looked like.

Turning the shower off and reaching for a towel to wrap myself in, I was sure I'd heard a knock on the door. "Harvey?" I asked, receiving no response.

I opened the bathroom door just in time to see Harvey

opening the front door and walking out to greet whoever was on the opposite side.

"Antônia in there?" Lorraine's voice was muted from outside. I gripped the towel tighter around my body and walked closer to the wall to hear better.

"She's in the shower," Harvey answered.

"Well, it's past checkout time, and her card bounced for the next payment. Let her know if she wants to keep her things, she needs to be out of here by one, or I'll be deactivating her key and tossing whatever's in the room in the trash."

"Okay."

Humiliation drenched my body with sweat, turning my shower useless. I ran back into the bathroom to hide, locking the door behind me and sitting on the toilet to brace for the upcoming meltdown.

It would have been hard enough to handle this situation on my own, but now that someone knew just how broke I was, all I could think about was shapeshifting into an ostrich and shoving my head into the ground.

I liked to keep my problems private, ingrained from my parents' upbringing of never asking for help, never showing weakness. Doing so only invited opportunities for our enemies to use our tears for fuel. So I kept all my troubles in my pocket, never truly opening my mouth to ask for the things I needed.

With good reason, too. Asking Lonnie for a job had turned into a bigger mess that I now needed to dig my way out of.

I stayed in the bathroom for far too long, waiting for my brain to tell my heart to calm down, to forget that the six dollars in my bank account wasn't even enough to have the lunch *I* had convinced Harvey to have with me. The clock hanging above the bathroom mirror read eleven twenty-five. It was earlier than I thought, but I had less than two hours to figure out the rest of my life now, two hours to find a place to keep my bags, two hours to decide if I'd be skating on Saturday or admitting defeat and calling my mother for a way to get to New York.

Mortified to leave the safety of the bathroom, my panic consumed me, every thought firing at rapid speed to the point where I couldn't keep up with a single one, just a cacophony of noise in my mind that overwhelmed me to the point of shutting down completely. Bringing my feet up to the closed toilet lid, I hugged my knees and lowered my head.

Maybe if I kept hiding, she'd just get tired of waiting and leave. Then I wouldn't have to face her, wouldn't have to deal with the awkward discomfort of the truth.

"You ready yet?" she shouted from the other side of the door.

Crap.

"No," I admitted, finally peeling my damp skin off the toilet lid and standing.

I adjusted my towel, wondering if pretending to be clueless was my best bet to get over this feeling.

"Oh shit, is that feijoada back there?" Harvey's voice came through louder.

I opened the bathroom door and peeked around the corner to see her rummaging through the mini fridge.

"You know what feijoada is?" I raised an eyebrow, running the brush over my hair.

"Hell yeah, I'd trade feijoada over any five-star meal. I had a girlfriend who was obsessed with Brazil, and she would make it all the time." Harvey groaned at the memory before looking up from the fridge with a grimace. "Shit... sorry, no one wants to hear about ex-girlfriends." She rubbed the back of her head awkwardly.

"Um...why would I care?" I worked through a knot, wincing as the brush snagged.

"I don't know, it's like a first date faux pas and whatnot," she said, opening the Tupperware and taking a sniff.

My stomach did a weird thing, sinking all the way down into my bowels, as if it could somehow escape through the back exit.

"Oh. *Oh.* Shit. Did you think this was a—" I stopped mid-sentence, unsure if her misunderstanding had been a cause of my own ignorance, my own inability to pick up on the social cues that were always obvious to everyone.

Everyone but me.

"Is this... not?" She was pink, biting her lip and fumbling with the right words to say.

"It's not you... I'm just not... gay," I confessed, and her eyes widened, like it wasn't the kind of rejection she was expecting.

She choked out a laugh. "Oh, sure. Okay." She shrugged, fighting back a knowing smile and stuffing her hands in her pockets.

"I'm not." I raised my eyebrows.

"I'm agreeing with you." She smirked.

"Satirically." I crossed my arms over my chest, her eyes staying locked on mine.

"No. If you're not gay, then who am I to say you are,

princess?" Her smile was borderline condescending, like this wasn't worth arguing about.

"So it's fine? Just like that?" I asked, for some reason not expecting the disappointment to wash over me like it did.

"Why wouldn't it be?" She shrugged again, this time looking away from me. "If this is awkward, I can just go?"

"I could still use a friend," I propositioned, unsure if it was a selfish request to ask for a friend when I'd clearly misled her into thinking we could be more. "Is that a lot to ask?"

She shook her head as she smiled again, this time more genuinely. "I wish we could stay in." She opened my fridge. "I can't stop thinking about that feijoada now."

I shook my head. "It's probably ancient," I confessed, not remembering when I had made it or when I had even put it in the fridge.

Had I driven into town with it?

Had my mother somehow found her way here? The brief thought planted its seed into my brain.

Harvey checked her watch anxiously, and had I not known Lorraine put a timeframe on my homelessness, my insecurities would have told me she was counting down the seconds to escape from here, to escape from *me*.

"Food?" she reminded me, pulling her phone out and not looking up from it. "My treat." She paused and glanced my way again. "Not a date," she clarified once more with a smile.

For some reason, this girl could say nearly anything, and it felt like the world was lifting off my shoulders. I didn't get it, but now, there was a newfound weight sitting on top of my chest. Something told me she wouldn't be able to help me with this one. I put on a pair of skinny jeans, knowing damn well they were out of style and that it gave off blaring sirens of my millennial identity. I forwent the bra and opted for a tight tank top, slipping on a *Gym class heroes* t-shirt that dated back to Warped Tour 2006.

I was in my own mental hell, held hostage between needing help and not wanting to tell anyone how badly I was struggling. Harvey seemed to have a small idea, but now it felt like a game of chicken. She hadn't mentioned Lorraine at the door, and there was no way in hell was I going to do it myself.

I sighed, slipping the backpack that carried my essentials over my shoulder and then reaching for my phone to thumb through the missed calls from the last thirty minutes.

"Grab all your stuff," she said, swiping her keys off the bedside table and heading for the door.

"Why?" I asked, though I knew the answer.

In an hour, all my things would be in the trash. I didn't even have a vehicle to store them in anymore, not unless I wanted to go down to East End garage and spend a fortune just to recover the waste of a shell that was my car.

She grumbled awkwardly, blowing air through her lips like she wasn't sure what to say. "Just do it, Nia."

She grabbed one of my still-closed suitcases and pulled it behind her as she exited the room. I scrambled, pulling my charger off the wall so fast, the USB cable came out of the plug still attached to the outlet. I only had a few dirty clothes randomly laid out on the floor. Picking them up and tossing them into my open suitcase, I did one final sweep in the bathroom for any rogue items I was guaranteed to leave behind.

A personal curse.

Tossing my derby duffle bag over my free shoulder and grabbing my backpack, I gave the room one final look before marching towards uncertainty.

What now?

I put aside my internal conflict for the day so I could at least enjoy my lunch. There was a new place in town that was apparently equal parts delicious and authentic, and that was absolutely unheard of in such a small town. My family had been the most ethnic thing in Devil Town until my mother decided she'd served her time, put in her notice at the local research facility that had sponsored my parent's immigration decades prior, and found a better job in New York.

One that didn't underpay her just because she was an immigrant and expected her to be grateful for what they gave.

A sign hung above a giant tree boasting the words *La Terazza* with an arrow pointing to the stairs. The place was whimsical, a three-story patio-treehouse hybrid with tables made of smaller tree trunks preserved in resin. Colorful tinsel cut into tiny little pieces hung from strings, lining the space above us like butterflies and traveling from branch to branch.

The smell of warm arepas invaded every one of my senses, forcing my mouth to water and my stomach to rumble. "This place looks amazing!" I couldn't hide my excitement, and with good reason. Nearly every table looked full, and on a weekday lunch in Devil Town? This place was clearly legit, a blessing to this little shit-hole.

"I don't know." Harvey cocked her chin to the side. "I'm still thinking about that feijoada." She threw a smirk my way before turning toward the hostess.

We settled for a table on the second-floor patio, and with heated lamps above us, it made for the perfect cozy, outdoor winter lunch. The blond-haired waiter clenched his teeth at our refusal of cocktails, the place apparently famous for their drinks. I'd worked as a server long enough to know that he thought us drinking water meant we were trying to keep the bill low, and keeping the bill low meant we wouldn't be tipping well.

"I can make it for you," I said halfway through my first bite of calamari.

"Huh?" she mumbled through a mouthful, not realizing I was still processing our conversation from before our first plates were served.

"Feijoada. You've done a lot for me while I've been here." I stabbed the fried little ringlet with my fork awkwardly and shrugged. "It's literally the least I could do to say thanks."

"Do not play with my heart right now, Nia." She dropped her fork to the plate dramatically and clutched her chest. "I will move mountains for the black beans."

I laughed, awkwardly covering my cheeks that felt swollen from the amount of laughing I'd done in her presence the last few days. "It's no biggie. I can swing it this weekend."

This weekend.

Even if it was only a couple days away, I was making long term plans now. As long term as it got for me, anyway. Since I'd gotten here, I had been taking each day in stride, never planning more than the next few hours. Now, I was planning to cook a meal for someone who was quickly becoming the best friend I'd never asked for.

The one I had always needed.

Would I be doing that Saturday before the bout? Would I be staying long enough to cook it on Sunday?

I reached for my phone to check for the tenth time today that the Sunday flight to New York was still available, and in the same movement, I hesitated, deciding to forgo it this once. Harvey caught the movement but didn't let any expression break through before picking up her utensils again.

Our forks clinked together as we both went for the last piece of the fried little squid rings.

How cliché, had this been an actual date.

She bit back a smile, and I would have bet my last six dollars she was on the same wavelength.

She had offered to go if it was too awkward, but every-thing about my life was just moving from one awkward moment to the next. Still, this wasn't—being here with her wasn't weird or uncomfortable, and I wanted her around. I didn't need to question my sexuality just because I wanted to spend time with a girl. I'd spent time with plenty of girls my entire life. That didn't mean I wanted to fuc—

"You can have it." She broke my inner monologue as if

she could see on my face that I was diving into identity crisis territory, freeing her fork from the calamari.

Before I could refuse, the waiter returned with the best looking arepas I'd seen outside of television. This wasn't Brazilian food, but I had yet to find any South American cuisine that wasn't to my taste.

I swallowed down the calamari and split an arepa in half, catching another side-eye from the barely-adult-looking server who once again tried for a cocktail upsell. I'd never stopped to think about how uncomfortable that would be for people in recovery, for those trying to stay sober, how much enjoyment of the day could be robbed by a simple thing like going out to eat and having someone constantly shove the Devil in your face and ask you to drink.

"We're good," I bit back with a little more sharpness this time. "Thank you." I finished with a smile to not come off as such a bitch.

"You don't have to do that," she said, picking up her glass for a sip of water.

"Alcohol is the only substance that makes people ask you why you *aren't* consuming it." I scrunched my nose. "How obnoxious would it be if he was asking us if we were *sure* we didn't want cheese every five minutes?"

Her laughter was contagious, making my cheeks hurt again as I fought the smile from spreading too wide. Her phone buzzed on the table, Nadine's name popping up and hardening all of Harvey's features. She didn't answer the call, nor did she wait for it to end before turning her phone off and sliding it into her pants pocket.

I was finally caught up.

I'd always been that way; just needed a little more help

to connect the dots than most. It was something I made light of in jokes and self-slander, as if I could help the way my brain did things.

If I made fun of myself first, then it wouldn't hurt so much when the others eventually did too.

"Are you... and... Nadine?" I hesitated even finishing the thought as I watched the creases in her eyebrows worsen.

She put her fork down, took a deep breath, and adjusted every single part of her body that was physically possible before she answered. "I'm me and Nadine is Nadine." She cut through each word as if they were bitter resting in her mouth.

"Sorry," I barely whispered, realizing I had touched something sensitive.

She let out an exhausted sigh. "No, I'm sorry. Nadine is great. I'm great. But together, yeah, we were pretty much the worst thing on this planet. Toxic, nonfunctioning, catastrophic kind of fucked up." She finally stabbed another arepa and put it in her mouth, chewing and swallowing before she continued. "We haven't been together for eight months now—*her* decision—but she still wants whatever she can get from me."

Whatever she could get from her?

"I wish I could say that doesn't sound healthy, but that would only make me a hypocrite." I let out a nervous laugh, taking a long sip of water to drown out the awkwardness in the air.

She didn't respond, didn't eat, just waited for me to elaborate.

"I don't know, kind of sounds like me and my mom." I gave an awkward grin, her face falling flat in disgust.

"Well, if our relationship hadn't already died a year ago, that comparison would have sure done it for me." She cringed, forcing out another laugh from me.

"My bad," I chuckled as a new server brought out the next set of small plates.

"I guess you pissed off the other guy," Harvey whispered behind her hand, as if it would keep the waitress from hearing her.

She laughed, telling us to enjoy our meal and walking back through the doors.

"Yes," I moaned, stabbing a perfectly fried half of a plantain with my fork and putting the entire thing in my mouth, folding it before using my fingers to shove it the rest of the way in.

"You've convinced me. You *aren't* gay," she said, a horrified look on her face.

"If I had a child, I would sell it for plantains," I clarified once I was able to swallow down the gigantic bite.

"Plátanos," she corrected me with a wink.

Was she getting back at me for the *Arctic Monkeys* thing? Too bad I was *never* wrong.

"Maybe here, *in this restaurant*," I whispered, "but my ancestors would rip me from the ground if I ever called their banana da terra a plátano. That's solely a Spanish speaker thing."

"Same fruit though?" Harvey asked.

"I mean, yes and no. It's kind of like asking if they'd consider the grapes the same in one area of France to another in Italy. Yes, but also no." I tried my best to explain, hoping I was making my grandmother proud from the beyond. "My mom used to say they limit American's reach of fruit species, that giving you all too many would be confusing."

"What, like we can't handle more than two bananas?" she chuckled out.

"Pandemonium," I said, making an explosion gesture with my hands and mimicking the sound.

"Honestly, that sounds about right. I'd probably lose my shit if I went to the store and had to pick between fifteen different bananas. I'd never leave." She nodded her head.

"See?" I gave my best all-knowing smirk.

She reached for an unused napkin, crumpling it into a loose ball in her hand before throwing it at me. I squealed, forcing multiple heads to turn in our direction, as if our joy was a bother to their meal.

We snickered, hiding behind the drink menu purposefully left on our table. Our new server noticed, and Harvey asked for the check, the awkwardness settling in again and sucking up the remainder of joy I'd just filled up on. I ached for the day money wouldn't have this effect on me, but the only solution to this feeling was more money. The only way to feel secure, to feel empowered on my own.

"You don't have to pay for me." I shook my head nervously as she pulled the checkbook from the center of the table and gave me a *"yeah, bullshit"* stare.

She hadn't called me out yet.

"I invited you, remember?" Her voice was flat, her annoyance growing.

"Actual–" I tried to clarify, but she cut in.

"Nia. *Stop.*" It was just one look.

One look that said, *drop this*. One look that said, *let me do this for you*. One look to keep my dignity intact. One look that was making me question my entire reality.

"I know I said we were taking the day off skating, but we gotta run by the track. Is that okay?" she asked, signing the bill and leaving our new waitress a generous tip.

I nodded, still a little frozen from the whiplash of the previous exchange but still following her down the tree-house steps, satisfied, full, and nowhere close to knowing what the future held for me.

CHAPTER 14

OUT OF BOUNDS

"Stay in the car." Harvey's demand came in the same tone as the one in the restaurant. The very same tone that tumbled through my stomach like winged bugs trapped in a jar.

"What?" I asked just in time for her to shut her car door, her back to me as she made her way inside the rink, no wallet, no gym bag, not even her phone in her hands.

She turned for just a split second, that same look forcing me to sink deeper into the passenger side seat, as if it could somehow consume me and swallow me whole. The look said, *I mean it*, but I was nothing if not a rebel, even in my late twenties. As soon as the double doors shut behind her, I was already unclipping my belt and reaching for the door handle.

It took five attempts to get it open on my own.

Skateland on a Thursday, two days before the bout, meant there was probably an official practice happening today, and neither of us were planning on being there.

Shit.

I scrambled out of the car, slowly opening one of the doors just enough to slide through without drawing any attention. There were only six or seven skaters I could see on the track, but it was early in the day. They were here out of dedication, not obligation. Harvey was already in the middle of them, demanding their attention and turning her back to me as I dove under the four-foot partition that separated the track from the rest of Skateland.

I couldn't hear anything past my heavy breathing, a mixture of my own nerves and adrenaline drumming through my ears with each heartbeat, only amplifying my internal noise. I stilled, taking measured, slow inhales until the pulsing dulled and my breath steadied again. That was when Harvey's voice became clear, the acoustics in the rink providing no privacy as long as it wasn't packed with bodies and music wasn't blasting.

"Tell Lonnie Green to get their ass out here," she shouted, sounding angrier than I'd ever heard her.

I heard Lonnie's stubborn huffing more clearly than my own thoughts, the slam of their apartment door loud as they stomped through the rink with shoes on.

Uh-oh.

"What the hell are you screaming for Cathrine Harvey?" Lonnie's abrasive use of her full name was startling, but the realization that Harvey had *not* been her first name was somehow even more shocking.

But now, I didn't have to go through the weirdness of asking her for it myself. Knowing it felt a little bit like a superpower. Hiding here felt like a huge violation of... something, but I couldn't not know.

"You want to tell me why you're extorting this girl for a

plane ticket when she's so broke, she doesn't even have a place to sleep tonight?" She was too loud, her tone too pissed, and I was now wishing I hadn't come inside at all.

Ostrich mode: activate.

Lonnie immediately shrank, and suddenly, I didn't want to be around to observe anyone's guilt or pity over my situation.

"Come into Lonnie's office with me, and I'll take your stitches out," Mercy whispered in my ear from behind, nearly evacuating my soul from my body from surprise.

But there she was once again, like a goddamn rider of Rohan, ready to save me.

I was mortified, caught snooping and poor: the worst combination.

I nodded my head and followed her, both of us running hunched over so we could remain behind the privacy of the half walls. Opening the door to Lonnie's office, Mercy threw the strap of her crossbody bag over her head and dumped it onto the desk. Without even looking my way, she slid the window open, projecting Harvey's voice straight into the little office booth.

She was helping me snoop.

She put her fingers to her lips, making a shushing gesture before she opened a package of sterile gloves and broke out her equipment. "Taking them out will be a lot easier. It just might feel weird, pulling," she warned.

I nodded, hopping up on Lonnie's table and getting an ear full of the conversation on the tracks.

"She needs a place to stay, Lonnie. She's fucking home-less because she's stayed here longer than she should have, and she has no way to get to where she needs to." I cringed, hating how many people were hearing those words, even if they were the truth.

"If Nia needed help, she'd tell me," Lonnie argued back, clearly not remembering how far my pride went.

"Would she?" Harvey asked again, crossing her arms.

"Okay, so she needs a place to stay. Then give her a place to stay," Lonnie yelled back, as if it wasn't any of their business. At the same time, Meredith (whose shirt actually said *Mercy-kill*) cut the thread of each stitch, one by one, little snips just above my ear that pebbled the flesh below my neck. "You think she wants to share my couch-bed with me and smoke cigarettes in the middle of the night? I don't know why you're making this my problem, Cath. I didn't take her money."

"You know exactly what you're doing, Lonnie. It's not fair," Harvey continued to stand up for me.

"You've known this girl for days. I've known her for years. You're right, I *do* know exactly what I'm doing. I'm helping her cut the chains her mom has had on her for the last decade." Lonnie's tone was softer now, like they meant it.

"What if she's not asking for your help?" Harvey's voice was almost hard to hear now.

"Then she shouldn't have come back here. It's the only thing I've ever been able to offer her." Lonnie turned away.

"She needs a place to stay!" Harvey yelled across the rink, letting every skater in the building know.

"Then give her a place to stay. Last I checked, you were the only one without three roommates, children, or living with your parents around here." They waved their hand in the air, dismissing Harvey's request.

And then began to step straight toward their office, where we were.

"We could always ask Nadine!" Lonnie added.

I shifted, uncomfortably anxious and ready to hide, but Mercy's firm grip on my head kept me in place.

"Two more stitches," she promised, but Lonnie was at best eight steps away from reaching us. "I'd offer you my mom's couch, but I don't think you want to drive an hour south with me every day until you leave."

I didn't answer. Didn't know what to say, didn't even know what to think. I hadn't asked anyone for help, and here they were, doing the one thing I hated most.

Pitying me.

I turned my head back to the window and, as if my stare alone had the power, Harvey's gaze turned in our direction, her eyes locking straight on mine. I didn't breathe.

Lonnie's voice cut in on our stare-off. "Oh. Guess you heard all that, then." They shrugged awkwardly. "Good; now I don't need to repeat myself. Get the hell out of my office, Mercy."

She cut the final stitch, giving me a nervous glance before sloppily shoving every item back into her bag and running out of the tiny room.

"Why didn't you tell me?" Lonnie's voice was soft now.

"Would it have mattered? Would it have made a differ-ence?" I looked down, avoiding any eye contact.

"Had I known you blew into town with pennies in your bank account? Yeah, it would have made a difference, Nia." Their tone was laced with frustration now, clearly directed at me.

"Do... Do you feel *bad*, Lonnie?" I asked, the right

corner of my lip curling at knowing that even after everything, Lonnie did still care, did still love me.

"Of course I feel bad, you little shit. You mean the world to me, regardless of... whatever that brain of yours tells you." They brushed me off, walking over to the counter and revealing a bowl with proving bread.

"I didn't tell you because it wasn't your problem." I crossed my arms, still trying to keep a shred of dignity intact.

"But it's Harvey's problem?" They seemed offended somehow that I'd trusted Harvey over them. Lonnie walked to the sink, washing their hands thoroughly while I attempted to remedy their ego.

I shook my head. "No, I didn't tell her. She was just at the right place at the right time."

"You're spending a lot of time together. I hope you're not here just to distract one of my best skaters and then leave another trail of wreckage behind you when you leave again." The words cut deep. They dried their hands before pulling the bubbly, raw dough ball out of the bowl and throwing it on the pre-floured counter.

"I don't even know what you're trying to say." I stood my ground, becoming defensive and genuinely clueless as to what they were accusing me of.

"Nadine's fucked with her head enough. Harvey doesn't need you using her for whatever bisexual awakening you've waited this long to have." The ridge between their eyebrows grew deep, and their words hit harder than a back block.

"I'm not fucking with anyone's head, *Lonnie*," I snapped back. "Does your concern come as someone who cares about her, or as someone who cares about winning on Saturday? Have you sent in the bets for the week yet?" I couldn't hold back anymore.

I had been the only one back then who knew Lonnie's secret, the gambling addiction that at times had almost cost us the entirety of the rink itself.

"I don't do that anymore." Their eyes narrowed my way, but their hands continued to work through the dough.

"That's why they left, isn't it? It wasn't about me leaving; it was about them finding out the truth, wasn't it? Does this new batch of skaters know?" I pressed, digging for more truths than I was sure I could even handle.

"I don't keep secrets anymore, Nia. Why don't you worry about your own problems instead of mine? Seems like you've got plenty of them." Lonnie turned their back to me, letting me know we were done.

I struck a nerve—the thing I was best at.

See, if I pushed Lonnie away, if I *forced* them to walk away first, then I could control the pain. It was better than waiting for the inevitable, for them to leave on their own once they got tired of me.

The walk around the track was excruciatingly long, the piercing heat of every skater's eyes uncomfortably following me as I made my way to the door. No relief settled into me once I reached outside, Harvey's face hard, eyes locked on me as she sat behind the wheel, waiting.

"I told you to wait out here." She sounded angry, but I wasn't even sure if it was at me.

"I-I'm sorry," I apologized, nervous, embarrassed, and full of self-loathing.

She shook her head. "No, no. Don't apologize. I just—"

"You were trying to protect me," I cut in, and she nodded. "I appreciate it."

"You can stay with me tonight if you want." She looked in my direction before starting her car. "I can sleep on the couch; you can have the bed."

"I will literally sleep on your bathroom floor before I take your bed away from you. Don't even try it." I turned the volume up, *The Black Keys* blaring at a volume I knew would be considered satisfactory by her standards.

She smirked before shifting the gear into reverse and pulling out.

"So," I said once we reached her door, not having spoken for the entirety of the ride back to her place. "Cathrine?" I dipped my toes in the water, checking the temperature.

Her head snapped my way so fast, I could almost hear it. "*Never* Cathrine," she warned. "Sometimes Cath, or Cat."

I smiled, glad she wasn't holding a grudge against me for listening in at the rink. "Kitty?" I teased.

She was most definitely *not* a Kitty.

She paused, her hand still on the keys, her stare burning into mine. "If a girl is calling me Kitty, she better be making me purr."

My mouth dropped open, and my face must have turned beet red, because it was on fucking fire. She pushed the door open, walking straight to her fridge and taking a pamphlet held down by a magnet. "Chinese tonight?" She tossed the menu my way before I'd even had a chance to sit down.

"You don't have to keep taking care of me. It's not even dinner time," I pointed out.

"What else are we supposed to do?" she asked.

She needed the distraction from drinking. I knew enough about recovery to know keeping busy was crucial; otherwise, the desire to drink could easily win.

"Do you have trimmers?" I asked, coming up with an idea.

"Yes," she said, suspicion lacing her tone as she dragged out the S.

"Now that my stitches are out, I need to fix whatever this is." I gestured to the half-assed shaved side of my head. "Can you help me?"

"You committing to the look?" She laughed, walking me toward her bathroom.

Bringing in a stool from her room, she plopped it in front of the mirror. "Sit," she said, commanding me down. "How much do you want off?" she asked, turning my head to the side so I could decide for myself.

My hair had been a point of pride for me. Long, strong, brown hair. The more classic the look, the more Latina I felt, which was hard to achieve some days. It was something my mother never understood, the feeling of not being enough to claim what you were.

I was born in Latin America, Antônia. Do you think people in Brazil sit around debating their latinidade? No, they just are, existing, next to each other. I don't think I even said the word latino until I moved to this country. You are just as Brazilian as I am, as your father is, and your grandparents before us. Don't let people who don't understand the sum of our experience try to define yours.

I craved that kind of confidence, that kind of right to my heritage.

"I don't know—shave the whole half." I shrugged.

Harvey's face brightened, shocked at my bravery. "You sure?" she asked, clicking the trimmer on. I nodded, taking a breath before leaning my head to the side and giving her room to work.

She started near the neck, and in a clean movement, she took the machine all the way around my ear and then, without a second of hesitation, continued to work. Her hand grazed my neck delicately in almost touches with every pass, sending goosebumps down my arms. In a few minutes, she had taken nearly half a head of hair off my scalp, the long, dark tresses spilled over the tile beneath us in a hairy mess.

"Welp, hope you like it," she said. "No going back now." She moved out of the way to show me the mirror.

It wasn't really half my head; she'd left a generous side part that cut right at my eyebrow, but everything below was gone. It was different, like nothing I'd ever done before, and right at this moment, it really suited me.

"So?" she asked anxiously.

"I love it!" I grinned, giving her a hug and draping her in excess hair. "Oh shit, my bad." I laughed nervously, slapping all of it off me and doing the same on her. She caught my hand at the wrist before I could brush any more off, holding it in place.

"Wash it off. I'll go get your bags out of the car and put them in my room so you can change."

I would have argued, said I could get them myself, but I was starting to learn that there wasn't much arguing with

Harvey, and I still felt guilty for following her into the rink. I agreed, but only after convincing her to at least let me clean up the aftermath on her bathroom floor.

"Can we talk about food yet?" she shouted from across the hall as I got ready in her room. "I'm starving."

I rummaged through my bag, finding a seemingly clean shirt and the sweatpants from the previous night. "I'll eat anything!" I yelled back, trying my best to be easy to deal with.

Then, I thought about Lonnie's words; they twisted and coiled around my mind even tighter than before, and I felt my lungs losing oxygen at the feeling. My breathing became shallower as I hyper fixated on every single word, every exchange, every accidental touch I might have somehow done over the last few days to give Harvey the wrong idea.

Was I using her? Not intentionally, and certainly not maliciously. But now that the thought had been planted in my brain, I couldn't overlook it, couldn't shut it out.

If anything, this would only further my obligation to the bout on Saturday, to pay back my debt.

Right?

I felt nauseous, anxious, heartburn radiating up to my throat now to the point where the idea of dinner was no longer on my radar.

"You look yellow. Are you okay?" She watched me from the other side of her open bedroom door, the dead-fish look on my face certainly enough to let her know something was wrong.

"I-I don't know if it's such a good idea I stay here, Harvey." I shook my head, gathering my things.

She laughed, watching me struggle with my duffel bag

and my rolling suitcase while I looked for my backpack. "Oh?" She crossed her arms over her chest, amusement so clearly outlined on her face. "Where will you be going?"

"I... I haven't thought that far yet, but I don't think I should stay here." I avoided her face as much as possible, looking at my hands, my feet, my suitcase, anything else but her.

"Okay, well, when you're done going through whatever... this is, I'll be in the living room." She gave me one final look before walking out of view in the hall.

Jesus Christ, did she just call my bluff? Was I bluffing, or did I just truly not have anywhere to go? I dropped to the bed with a groan, reaching for my phone in the backpack and thumbing through the notifications.

Maybe a sign of life would ease this feeling, this guilt I couldn't label but also couldn't shake off. I sent the text to my mother:

> I'LL BE LEAVING DEVIL TOWN IN THE NEXT FEW DAYS.

> BEIJOS

The call was almost immediate, my stomach churning uncomfortably in anticipation, and there I was, regressing again, hiding from my mother because the confrontation was still something I couldn't deal with, couldn't handle on my own. When I was younger, I would go running under

Lonnie's wing, waiting for them to lend me their courage, and we would take these calls together. They held my hand, squeezed tight, and reminded me that my mother's words were the only weapon she had against me, and that it was up to me to decide how sharp they were.

I'd never learned to put on my armor, and her weapons became razor-edged with time.

"I've been calling you all fucking day. What gives, Cath?" Nadine's voice was abrasive and loud, and the slam of the door behind her was strong enough to feel in the room.

Well, I guess I definitely wasn't leaving *now*.

"I've been busy." Harvey's voice was flat, bored, like she didn't care to put any emotion in answering Nadine.

"Busy avoiding practice? Or busy avoiding me?" I felt grosser listening to this conversation than the one at the rink. This wasn't meant for me, and here I was, not having any control over whether I'd be forced to hear it.

"Definitely avoiding you. *Not* avoiding practice. I've skated every day this week, unlike *you*." The silence was unbearably long and I held my breath, just wanting the awkwardness of this moment to end.

"Is someone else here?" she asked, her tone becoming angrier by the minute.

My backpack.

"Yup," Harvey answered, no inflection again.

"Will you put the goddamn remote down and look at me?" Nadine screamed, but Harvey didn't bother answering. A shrill noise came from the living room and then heavy stomping of feet followed.

Each step got closer to the room until I had no choice

but to look up from my hands, to find Nadine staring daggers straight into me.

"Nice. Real fucking nice." She snorted, turning on her heels and marching away.

"Call your girlfriend," Harvey tossed out casually.

Another loud slam of the door let me know she was gone, but it didn't ease the feeling in my chest at all. I wasn't responsible for whatever was happening between them; hell, I wasn't even responsible for whatever she thought was happening between us.

There's nothing happening between us. I silenced my inner thoughts before they could consume me.

I waited a few minutes, the longest of my entire life, before I decided to come out of her room. Harvey was propped up on her couch, one foot on the ground and the other on the cushion, her knee bent and her arm casually resting on it while she ate a bag of Skittles, nonchalant as hell, as if she hadn't just been terrorized by the redhead.

"If you're still leaving, I'd wait a bit." She laughed. "Nadine is probably waiting outside for you."

My heart sank, my face feeling flush. "Why?"

"You know why." She threw a look my way that said *don't play stupid.*

"But I'm not gay. I would have told her that. Why didn't you tell her that?" I asked, almost upset that I was somehow entangled in this thing that wasn't even my business.

"Because it doesn't matter. You have nothing to do with me and Nadine. We've been done for a long time. She needs to stop relying on me to fix her problems." She popped a handful of Skittles into her mouth. "But you can declare your heterosexuality out the window for her if you need to." She laughed again. "I'm sure she'll appreciate it."

"That was so awkward." I slumped down on her couch.

"Sorry." She shrugged, really not seeming to care about Nadine's opinion on the situation.

"I don't think she'll want to skate with me Saturday." I grimaced.

"She's a weak blocker. Mo will probably bench her if you're jammer." She picked the menu off the table again.

For some reason, the thought wasn't comforting. I wasn't here to take anyone's place.

"We're still assuming I pass my skills test tomorrow," I added, less hopeful than ever before.

"Do it first thing in the morning, while you still have energy." She handed me the pamphlet. "What do you like?"

"I'm a sucker for egg drop soup. Anything else is a bonus." I gave it back to her, not wanting to be picky.

She rolled her eyes like she could see through me, and dialed the number on her phone, tossing me the remote and nodding to the TV. I flicked through the options on the streaming service, looking for anything easy to tune out but finding the options overwhelming and anxiety inducing. I scrolled to her "continue watching" section and opted for a show about aliens on our planet.

The food came fast, but then again, Devil Town only took ten to fifteen minutes to cross from any part of the city. We ate on the coffee table, both of us overly focused on Giorgio Tsoukalos and his attempts to convince us that the Anunaki were real.

She ordered too much, but apparently, that was the way she preferred it. "I'm always thinking about later food." She shrugged, happily packing the leftovers into the fridge after we'd stuffed ourselves with sesame chicken and crab wontons.

"You're well prepared. I'm literally never thinking more than five minutes into the future," I explained.

"Is that why you've been ready to leave since the minute you got here?" She raised an eyebrow, sitting back on the couch next to me.

"It's easier to pretend I'm desperate to leave than to admit how badly I'd rather just stay. This town is the only place I ever called home." The truth came out too easily, making me far more vulnerable than I knew I had the right to be.

"Are you leaving for you, or are you leaving for your mother?" She was better at digging things out of me than Lonnie, and I had considered their skills unmatched.

"I'm not ready to answer that," I groaned, slamming my back into her couch and doing my best to become one with the furniture.

"My bad," she laughed, throwing her hands up in the air. "No more prodding, I promise."

"You're really good at asking all the questions I've been refusing to answer," I told her. "It's only slightly annoying." I bit back a smile, but a yawn fought its way out of me instead. "Oh shit. Off-days are more tiring than skate days."

Something about taking it easy just made it so I wanted to sleep all day and rest, made me want to lean into the fatigue and just rot in a little ball of blankets for an entire week. Harvey was in the same place as I was, and it was the tiny twitch of her head nodding down that let me know she was done for the day too.

"Let me go get the bed ready for you," she mumbled, and I knew we'd be having it out to see who'd be sleeping on the couch tonight.

Another sacrifice I refused to let her make for me. I closed my eyes and faked a snore.

"You're a pain in the ass. Get up." She shook me, laughing as she tried to get me to drop my pretense.

I snored louder, letting my head fall to her shoulder for drama.

She grumbled, "Fine. When you wake up uncomfortable, you can change your mind." Squinting through barely open eyes, I watched as she crossed her arms over her chest and dropped her head back to sleep.

This was a game of chicken I could win—I was sure of it.

I yawned again, this time letting sleep take me.

She was right: I was uncomfortable as hell when my body woke me in the middle of the night, sore and desperate to stretch. I laid myself down on the couch, curling into my side as I cozied up to sleep once again.

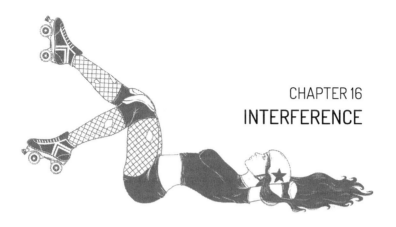

F alling asleep with my mouth open was always the worst. A puddle of drool gathered under my cheek, and I wiped away at it with the back of my arm. Stretching wide with my elbows out, I rubbed at my eyes, finally opening them slowly to the daylight in the room. Harvey stared down at me, a far more alert look in her eyes, like she'd been awake for a while now.

And my head was on her lap.

Oh f—

I scrambled to sit, attempting to wipe the drool off my face but only spreading it around further. She bit back a laugh watching me.

"I'm *so* sorry!" I backed into the furthest side of the couch, cursing at myself and drowning in embarrassment.

"For what?" She lifted a shoulder, unbothered that I'd used her lap as a pillow all night. Changing the subject, she asked, "Do you want to eat before you test?"

She was good at that, at knowing when to move on

when something made me too uncomfortable to linger in the feeling.

I looked over to the kitchen clock—it was ten in the morning, far later than I expected. I seemed to be sleeping a lot lately, maybe due to the head injury, but I couldn't spend too much time worrying about the possible repercussions of that going unchecked. It would need to get in line with the rest of my problems.

"No, if I eat now, it'll just slow me down." I stood, heading into the bedroom to grab my skate bag. "Plus there's a ninety-eight percent chance I'm going to puke."

"Fair." She nodded as I filled up my water bottle with fresh ice. "Write me a list of what you need, and I'll grab it from the store after practice."

"What I need?" I asked, her thoughts not in line with my own.

"For the feijoada. You're crazy if you think you're leaving here without letting me eat your beans." She grinned the minute the words left her mouth.

"Why does that sound so *wrong* when you say it?" I bit the inside of my cheek.

"It's truly a skill." She winked as we made our way out of her apartment and headed for Skateland.

"Remind me to tell you what it means someday." I held back my smile.

"Wait, what?" She pulled at my arm, and I turned my gaze in her direction, shaking my head.

"Don't worry about it." I broke free from her grasp and made my way inside the car, knowing damn well she wouldn't be satisfied with that answer.

The rink was packed, irritatingly enough, for no other reason than for my skills test. Every skater in the Devil's Dame Derby league made it out to show their support. Well, everyone but Nadine, but I didn't blame her for not sharing their enthusiasm. It was more than I deserved, and the guilt overwhelmed me more than their kindness did.

I took my time changing in the locker room, putting on a pair of neon blue panty hose under tight spandex shorts and slipping on a black crop top over my sports bra. I pulled the brush out of my bag and ran it through my hair a few times before braiding it down the side and tossing it over my shoulder.

One by one, I put on each piece of protective gear: first the helmet, then the pads, and then lastly, my skates. I took one final look in the mirror and decided to let go of it all—all the thoughts, worries, and what ifs that still hung in the air. I would simply live in the moment and just enjoy the gift of being able to skate once again.

If I passed, then great, but if I didn't, then maybe that was the sign I truly needed to move on.

Using my mouth to tighten my wrist guard, I took one final look in the mirror. Deep breaths. Rolling my shoulders back with my exhale, I took off toward the track.

Mo skated out to the center of the track, tying their brown hair into a ponytail at the top of their head before blowing the whistle. "They do not fuck around, do they?" I chuckled, looking over to Mercy.

"They're stricter than Lonnie," she warned me.

Mo blew the whistle again, breaking me out of my trance just as Mercy pushed me dead center in the back, forcing me into position on the track.

"Who are you skating with?" Mo asked me again, just as they had the first time.

I shook my head, once again refusing to condemn someone to starting their day with skating twenty-seven laps in under... "Is it five minutes or four?"

"Five. What the hell kind of crazy shit was Lonnie having you all do before?" Mo shook their head.

"It was intense back then." I laughed, coming up onto my toe stops behind the blue line and bending my knees.

"When you're ready." Mo gave me the warning, and I nodded in their direction. The countdown to three came first, and then another whistle before I began to move.

It felt better this time, lighter and easier to give my all without having burnt most of my energy skating half the day away. I didn't bother to conserve it, knowing I didn't have the luxury of *not* making it.

My lungs were on fire by the ninth lap, but my legs still felt good under me. My skates were solid, each truck perfectly tuned on its plate, giving me the most stable footing to go on. I pounded the track, every crossover tighter than the last as I held my wrists behind my back to really hug the curves.

It was unbearably loud, every single skater screaming my name or a form of encouragement to cheer me on.

Eleven.

Lonnie's face blurred in the distance, with a smile of approval as I crossed the line once again.

Thirteen.

Remember to breathe, I chanted in the back of my head, the sweat dripping off my nose in microbeads.

Fifteen. Every lap got harder than the last, and the thought that I wouldn't make it once again began to take root in my mind.

Quiet. I told my brain, hearing nothing but my skates against the waxed track once more.

I lost count, turning my head to the side to check Mo's face for any tell of time left.

I pushed forward, but there wasn't anything left to give, no leftover energy to propel me, no chance to move my legs any faster.

The voices in the distance became pleas instead of cheers, hope leaking out of me for any likelihood of making it. I had wanted a sign, and here it was.

Skates battered behind me in a thunderous cascade, and before I'd gotten a chance to turn my head back, Harvey, Mercy, and Ash had entered the track, passing me with ease.

Giving me a goal. Giving me exactly what I needed to finish.

I moved faster than before, a second wind showering me with the boost to push my body past the breaking point. Every inch of me was on fire, sweat dripping from every pore, from my fingertips down to my legs.

"Move!" Mercy shouted from ahead, and I shortened my crossovers, taking the next turn even sharper, passing her from the left and crossing the line.

I wasn't going to make it. For some reason, the longer I skated, the further I felt from twenty-seven laps, and without the blow of the whistle, I had no idea what would come first: the end of the timer, or me.

The mixture of belligerent screams calling out my name, telling me to go, and obscenities were impossible to tell apart. Instead, I used them as fuel to move my skates just another few inches, and when those wheels hit that blue line, Mad Morgan finally blew their whistle.

My body shut down. I dropped to my kneepads and slid the next few feet across the waxed rink before slumping down face first.

I heaved uncontrollable gasps before Mercy grabbed me by the collar of my shirt and turned me on my back to catch a full inhale. Nausea swept through me like a current, washing away every thought and feeling in me aside from the need to purge.

"Big breaths through your nose," Mercy instructed. "Out through your mouth."

I exhaled hot spurts of air, each one cooling my body down significantly until the urge to vomit passed.

"Did I do it?" I asked through labored breaths, keeping my eyes closed to protect from the salt of my sweat-drenched skin.

"You did it." Harvey's voice had never been so comforting than it was in that moment.

My chest vibrated, and every emotion poured out of me in the form of exhaustive tears.

"Give her some space!" Mo's voice came from the distance, and when I opened my eyes, I found almost every member of the Devil's Dame Derby League staring back at me.

I was one of them again.

And it felt even better than I expected.

L onnie was the first to break through the wall of skaters, squeezing me tight, clearly unbothered by how sweaty or smelly I was as they lifted me into the air for a hug.

"Lonnie," I wheezed out, "I'm gonna puke." I was over the worst of it, but if they kept crushing me, there was a good chance I wouldn't be in control anymore.

"Put her down!" Mo shouted, but the minute my wheels hit the ground, I was dogpiled on by every skater around me.

First, Mercy and Trixie, then Ash, Angelina and Jackie, and then those whose names I couldn't remember yet.

Yet.

"Give the girl some space." Harvey's voice came from somewhere outside the pile where I was slowly suffocating.

The happiest death of my life.

"What? So only you can smother her–ow!" Trixie's comment made me laugh a pained wheeze as my lungs fought for reprieve.

I dug out as if I was crawling out of my own tomb, my hand sticking through the only hole I could find bathed in the smallest stream of light. A hand gripped my wrist, pulling me out of the mess of bodies until I was finally freed from the mountain of skaters. Gasping, I filled my lungs with air, crashing onto Harvey on the ground.

I turned to face her, only to find a giant smile plastered on her face, like she was just as proud as I was.

"Great job, champ," she teased. That devilish grin never looked so good on her face.

"Thank you," I mouthed. "Seriously."

I wasn't thanking her for congratulating me.

"I would have done it before had you just asked." She shrugged. "But you're not an asker, are you?"

I shook my head.

"I can't read your mind." She grinned.

"Pity. It's wildly entertaining in here." I shoved her away just in time for a foot to drop between our faces, the tangle of bodies slowly coming undone as they realized I'd snuck my way out of their human pretzel ball.

The whistle blew again, practically in my ear this time as Lonnie pushed their way out of the pile, demanding order. "All right, All right," they yelled. "Nia, go stretch. Then go home and rest–" They stopped, remembering I had no home before stumbling through the next few words. "Catch a break. Everyone back here at six for scrimmage before the bout. It's slam night tomorrow, Devils."

I snowplowed my way into a corner far from the other skaters, where I could stretch my already throbbing muscles. Leaning on the ground with my legs in a pigeon pose, I groaned, feeling every ligament, every pull of my hamstring. I stayed on the right side longer than normal, really working out the lactic acid.

"What's your plan for the day?" Trixie asked as she came to a hockey stop inches away from my face.

"I don't know. This was about as far as I'd gotten for today. I figured I'd hang out around here, maybe do some drills until practice later. I'm sure Harvey could use a break from me being in her space." I shrugged.

"Is that what she said?" Trixie looked around, as if in search of Harvey for confirmation. "That doesn't sound like her."

"No, but I'm exhausting to deal with." I switched sides, bending my left leg into the same stretch.

Everything about me felt tiresome, too much to be burdened by. I couldn't make my entire existence the responsibility of someone who had already made it clear she was shit at boundaries, incapable of turning down someone in need, so self-sacrificing it was borderline dangerous. The less I appeared in need of her help, her time, her presence, the better.

Despite how clearly I was drawn to it.

"Hmm, well. Come swimming then." She tossed out the invitation too casually.

"Swim? In the middle of winter? Are you insane?" I laughed.

"At Freyer's hole. You said these were your stomping grounds, right?" she questioned, as if I didn't know this town like the back of my hand.

Freyer's hole was a hot spring hidden in the middle of the only mountain peak in Devil Town. It was a small hike past the fenced off area in the park, where it was most definitely not legal to cross and especially not legal to swim.

But the locals didn't care, and they weren't shelling out enough government money to the city to hire a park ranger or anyone who would actually patrol those areas and keep the kids out.

I hadn't swum there in ages. I was nineteen the last time I chanced it, and two weeks after, a girl from my graduating class ended up in the news dead from it. It was nothing wild; she just slipped on a wet rock and hit her head, and because she had gone alone, she drowned.

After that, my friends and I kept our distance, the small grains of worry that build with time and age set into our bones, making us feel too old to take the risk.

"Sure," I agreed, deciding that if I was going to say goodbye to this place,

I'd better do it right. "I just gotta go to Harvey's and grab some swim stuff."

She stuck her hand out for me to grab, helping me to a stand on my skates. "Come on, I'll drive you over there."

"Did she already leave?" I nearly broke my head off my neck twisting it around to search for her face in the crowd.

"Yeah, Nadine summoned her like five minutes ago to take her to work. Harvey asked me to give you a ride, so I figured we could make a day of it." She led in front as we joined the rest of the skaters on the bench, undoing our laces and taking off all our gear.

More than half the skaters had their quads on, and considering we were only here for me to take my minimum requirement test, it made me wonder just how many of them had planned to join me on that track. The feeling was too good, too pure, too warm and overwhelming to linger on.

"Does she always do that?" I asked, unsure if it was even my business to know.

"Who? Nadine? Or Harvey?" she asked loudly, her voice full of amusement. "Nadine is only up her ass right now because all of Harvey's attention is on you. She's been sleeping with Jackie for at least three months now."

It was more information than I could process at once. Once again, the confirmation of Harvey's attention on me, too obvious for anyone to ignore, made me feel like I'd been leading her on. The worst part was, I wasn't even sure I didn't want it, that I didn't enjoy it, and that I wasn't now craving it. It was enervating, pretending like I didn't immediately search for her the minute I entered a room, or that her presence had become enough to calm any sort of existential dread that bubbled up in my soul.

Being around Cat Harvey was like drinking a Valium tonic after swallowing an ecstasy pill. Lethal, dangerous, but the drop was bliss.

I shook the thought out of my head, telling myself that an afternoon away was exactly what I needed to clear my brain. Maybe even a call to my mother would beat the sense back into me.

Mercy joined us, claiming she rarely went anywhere without her derby-wife, a position Vominatrix was more than happy to fulfill. The stop at Harvey's apartment was brief, the spare key exactly where they'd left it the night of the party, but the place itself was empty, like Harvey had yet to come home.

I packed a few extra outfits into my backpack before

changing into a bikini under my regular clothes. Tying my hair up into a giant topknot above my head and a half glance at the mirror was all I required before locking up Harvey's place and getting back into Trixie's car.

"Ash is gonna meet us at Freyer's," Mercy said without looking up from her phone.

The drive was filled with loud music and even louder chatting. The overwhelming feeling of rightness all around me. Every second I spent with these girls was bringing me back to life, like being pulled from the ocean and being forced to breathe air.

It didn't take long to arrive, Ash was already waiting for us with the girl I'd known as *Jackie The Rip-her*.

Nadine's girlfriend.

Part of me expected to see Nadine coming out of the car as well, and when only the two of them appeared, I found myself able to relax, unsure why I even felt so uneasy at just the idea of her when I'd done nothing wrong.

Mercy chuckled under her breath, like she'd noticed my composure failing, "What?" I turned her way.

She shook her head, but Trixie answered for her. "It's just funny that you're more comfortable around one of Harvey's exes than the other." She bit the tip of her tongue under a smile, scrunching her nose at me.

I froze, trying to make sense of what she was saying, but neither of them stopped to wait for me as they waved the girls down.

"Wait, what do you mean, *one* of them?" I struggled to catch up, squeezing between them and trying to get answers before we'd reached Jackie and Ash. "Nadine *and* Jackie?" I asked. "They're both Harvey's exes?"

Mercy nodded, like it was the most casual thing ever.

"And now they're dating each other?" I clarified the final bit of information I'd been given, just to make sure I wasn't missing anything.

"Yup." Trixie popped the P casually.

"To be fair, she and Jackie dated like three years ago." Mercy rolled her eyes at Trixie, as if the information wasn't even relevant anymore.

Just as we reached the two girls, Jackie leaped toward me, giving me a big hug and congratulating me on passing my skills test, since she hadn't gotten a chance to do it at the rink.

We condensed all our things into one giant bag, Ash volunteering to carry it during the hike and not taking no for an answer. Freyer's Park was the only piece of untouched nature left in Devil Town, and viewing it from above, it was easy to fall in love with this little piece of land again.

It was beautiful, even with all the foliage dead and the thick blanket of winter draped over the ground. It was the kind of magical peace that made you believe in miracles, seeing everything below you.

We passed the "No entry" sign and found the hole in the wire fence someone had cut generations before us. I took the bag from Ash while she got through and then lifted it over the top when it was my turn.

I was sweating by the time we actually made it to the springs, forgetting with time the effort it took to get to this little hidden slice of paradise, and definitely in far worse shape than any previous time before. I removed every single layer down to my bikini top, holding my shirt and my sweater in my hands along with the rest of the girls, who had shed theirs throughout the trek.

The little cavern revealed itself to us, a small ledge just beneath our feet that we had to climb down to in order to access the entrance. It was possibly the most dangerous part of the entire journey, since the wrong footing could mean falling fifty feet into nothing but rocks and fallen boulders. One by one, we helped each other down until we'd all reached the steamy cave, the heat from the natural springs creating humidity that didn't exist this time of year.

Trixie and Mercy ran through the cave holding hands, only letting go to jump into the bright blue pool of hot water. It was clearer than I remembered, but the cave itself remained unchanged. My initials were somewhere on the wall, along with fifteen hundred others who thought they were leaving their mark on the world here.

The water was heavenly, equal parts soothing and just hot enough to ease every angry muscle in my body. A bath was everything I'd been craving that I couldn't have in Lorraine's Motel's standing shower.

Conversations swirled around me while I closed my eyes and rested my head on a nearby rock, dissociating fully into the calm the water provided me.

"I heard Nadine kind of laid into you yesterday?" Jackie's voice forced my eyes back open.

"I wouldn't say that... exactly." I grimaced. She'd only said a few words to me, and granted, now that I knew she'd had a girlfriend the entire time, I wasn't sure I even felt bad for any of it anymore.

I didn't even have the screaming urge anymore to explain that Harvey and I weren't a thing.

"Still, she shouldn't have said anything to you," Trixie assured, like I'd needed comfort from the exchange.

"Did she tell you?" I asked Jackie, but she shook her head with a laugh.

"No, we aren't *that* serious. Harvey called me this morning, though. She won't bother you anymore. She's just kind of... going through some things." She gave me an awkward smile.

"She didn't bother me," I promised, feeling kind of sorry for her.

I could see why it would be hard to get over someone like Harvey, someone who gave you that much attention, that much care.

That kind of love would be intoxicating.

Impossible to recover from.

I'd run away from it my entire life, never dating a guy for more than two or three months, always detaching the moment they'd cling to me, professing their love or obsession. When the chase ended, so did my attention span.

"I brought party favors." Ash perked up, lifting out of the water and padding toward her bag.

Rummaging through it for a few seconds, she raised her fist in victory before running back to the water with a flask in each hand. The girls clapped as she jumped into the spring, keeping both fists raised above the water the entire time.

She took a swig of each one, handing one off to her left and then the other to her right.

It was such a small flutter in my heart, but there was something about this moment right here, right now. I felt intrepid, armored with love and a feeling of family I'd been missing for so long.

For girlhood, for sisterhood, for softness and laughter.

Everything I had desperately been searching for, but never brave enough to say out loud.

"We're glad you're here, Nia." Jackie raised a flask to cheers, a hiccup falling from her mouth as the others joined in laughter.

"It feels good to be here," I admitted, but the bigger truth was, it felt good to be *wanted*, to be *welcomed*.

After spending the majority of my life on the outside and giving up the one thing that had made me feel connected to something, had made me feel whole, I didn't expect to come back and find that, even without the people from before, I could still feel the same joy, love, and happiness here.

That hadn't been part of my plan at all.

"Don't we still have scrimmage tonight?" The words slurred out of me as we tossed the empty flasks to the side, the heat of the springs only intensifying my buzz.

"Better not tell Lonnie. They'll kick all our asses," Trixie cackled.

"Four hours to sober up," Mercy declared, looking at her watch.

"Who's gonna drive?" Ash busted out laughing, but we all quieted at the realization, looking at each other and concluding every single one of us was a step down from being drunk.

We all laughed again, Mercy reaching behind her for her phone and shushing us as she dialed on speaker.

"Hello?" Harvey's voice was clear and sober, and my heart thundered in my throat.

"Elllerrr," Mercy slurred, and the rest of the girls giggled.

"What?" she asked, seemingly annoyed at the phone call already.

"We're stuck. Please come get us, Daddy." They all burst out in laughter again, and Harvey's grunt came through the speaker with silence.

"It's not my fault you're idiots. Call someone else." She groaned in frustration, but just as it seemed she was about to hang up, Trixie cut in from beside her. "Nia's with us."

There was a long pause on the other end, and then a small exhale. "I'll call you when I'm above the ledge."

W e'd been giggling like drunk fools since the minute Harvey hung up. The girls were now taking bets on whether Harvey was going to be calling us idiots at least three more times, or just dumbasses once from the get-go.

"She acts like she's bothered, but I think she'd lose it if she wasn't taking care of someone." Trixie stumbled through each word but looked damn proud of herself once she'd realized she'd gotten through the entire sentence coherently.

"Who takes care of her, then?" I asked, slipping my clothes on over my dripping wet swimsuit.

They all kind of looked at each other, as if no one had ever asked that question before.

"Hey, Dumbasses," Harvey called from outside the cave, interrupting the short moment of seriousness before we all cracked up again.

"You came for us!" Mercy squealed, running to the

mouth of the cave, where her legs eventually disappeared from sight, like she'd been pulled from above.

One by one, each girl scurried their way out, receiving an earful from Harvey, who still lifted them onto the ledge and to safety. I stood to the side, awkwardly waiting my turn. "You comin'?" She peaked her head down from the ledge when I didn't step out on my own.

I nodded, nervously approaching the opening. I'd done this tons of times as a teenager, but I'd never been brave enough to do it intoxicated, old wisdom imparted by the drug dealer I'd lived with for a short time. Something about only breaking one law at a time, and though I was sure those weren't his exact words, the meaning was essentially the same.

Only one dumb idea at once.

It kept me alive this long, so I couldn't claim it wasn't good advice.

The annoyed look on her face turned into amusement once she saw me, dishing a smile my way and softening her expression. "Put your foot on that ledge." She gestured with her head as she reached her hand out to me. "Then give me your hand."

I obeyed, carefully wedging my foot into the small lip on a rock that gave me just enough footing for her to lift my body to the safety of the mountain again. She rolled me off her while steadying me.

Now that we were out of the cave, I could feel I was far more drunk than I had realized.

She looked between the five of us, shaking her head before she opened her mouth. "Don't let these bad influences corrupt you, Nia." She turned to the rest of them. "You're lucky Lonnie's gone until Sunday."

"Wait, what?" I asked, feeling a little betrayed that they hadn't let me in on their plans to not attend the bout they'd made all this effort for me to skate in.

"Their mom is dying. She only has a week or so left, if that," Harvey explained as we hiked back toward the car, the wetness of the bikini under my clothes slowly drenching me from the inside out.

I couldn't remember Lonnie mentioning a problem with their mom, but then again, I hadn't asked either. Had I parentified Lonnie so much that they didn't feel comfortable relinquishing their burdens to me anymore?

The realization stung more than the sharpness of the cold wind against my now completely wet clothes, my teeth chattering as we descended from the mountain into the parking lot.

We packed into Harvey's car, the other four girls making no objection to squeezing in the back once they'd heard I was an easy puker.

"Thanks for the ride, Dad," Mercy blurted out as soon as we took off, earning herself a look from Harvey through the rearview mirror that had me sinking deeper into my seat but had the rest of the girls laughing even harder.

We only drove a few short minutes before pulling up to a small house just on the edge of town that was apparently where Trixie's family lived. "You can all get out," Harvey announced, turning her music down for the first time since the dad joke. Jackie and Ash grumbled about being nowhere near their homes but were only met with a dismissive wave from our driver. "Not my problem. Find your own way home," she declared as they emptied the car.

I reached for the handle of my own door, wiggling it once, then twice, giving up on the third. She reached over me, the smell of apricots invading my senses as she grabbed the handle and pulled the door open so I could leave.

"Are you mad?" I bit my lip, avoiding her gaze as I waited for the response.

She huffed in amusement. "Not at all, I'm just not going to babysit those idiots until scrimmage tonight. Do you want to stay with them?"

"Oh shit." I hiccuped, shaking my head. "Can I come with you?" I hiccuped again, realizing I was probably hours from that and likely still getting drunker by the minute with how fast we downed all the whiskey in those flasks. "I need to sober up."

"Yeah." She let out a full laugh, closing my door and leaning back before putting the car in reverse. "That's not happening for a while." She glanced my way before fixing her eyes back on the road. "I'll make you some coffee."

"That doesn't actually make you sober," I slurred, still correcting her despite my drunken state.

"You don't sound very convincing." She smirked.

"When I was in high school." I put more effort into each word so she wouldn't make fun of me. "I got *really* drunk before a basketball game with a few other girls, like four of us sharing a liter of vodka, maybe four hundred pounds between us all. Anyway, I blacked out, woke up at home under the shower with my grandmother praying over me in Portuguese while my mother forced hot coffee down my throat." I chuckled at the memory.

"Jesus Christ." She looked at me in shock.

"I heard the other girls got their stomachs pumped, but I spent two days throwing up at home. The luxuries of not being white. My parents were terrified to take a minor to the hospital for alcohol poisoning and risk deportation." The memory would have sobered me up if it could have. Had I understood then what I knew now about the weight of our existence in this country, things might have been a little different.

"So, trauma coffee's out, then." She confirmed nervously as she reached over to open my door once we'd arrived at her apartment again.

"I probably just need to sleep it off," I admitted, kicking my shoes the minute we entered her place.

"Some food would help," Harvey suggested, walking toward the kitchen.

But my teeth were chattering, and all I could focus on was taking off my layers and putting on something dry. I slipped the sweater off and dropped the pants to the ground, bending down to pick them up before walking toward Harvey's room.

The sound of her throat clearing uncomfortably from the kitchen reminded me I hadn't been alone, but my give a fuck meter was low. Whiskey only made it lower.

I'd somehow managed to stumble into dry and clean sweats without breaking anything in Harvey's room, though not for lack of trying. I had fallen at least three times just trying to get underwear on.

"Feel free to nap on the bed," she called from the living room, but I was already walking in that direction.

Always gravitating toward her.

She was, once again, perched on her favorite end of the couch, one foot up while she snacked on a blurry bag of cheese puffs. She raised an eyebrow once she found me standing at the edge of the hallway, staring.

"Can we watch the alien show again?" I asked. "I'm avoiding being alone with my thoughts."

"Mmm." She nodded. "Welcome to the club." She pointed to the cushion next to her.

I dropped down, pulling my feet under me and settling in next to her. Less than ten minutes of conspiracy theories had gone by before my eyelids drooped and my head jerked from the pull of gravity.

I leaned into her, dropping my head to her shoulder and closing my eyes.

"Nia." She said my name so softly, like trying to wake me up without actually waking me up.

"Hmm?" I grumbled, the pull of drunken sleep too heavy to ignore.

"What are you doing?" she whispered.

"Sleeping it off," I groaned.

"Um, maybe you should go take the bed," she suggested, less whisper in her voice this time, though her tone was still gentle.

"I'm so comfy," I whined, sliding down to her lap and reaching the point in drunken exhaustion where I would probably start getting violent soon if she didn't let me pass out.

"Look, I'm trying to believe you when you tell me one thing, but then you act like something else entirely." She wasn't quiet anymore, but her words weren't making sense.

"What?" I opened my eyes only to find the room had doubled.

"Just sleep it off." She sighed exhaustedly, a tug in my chest feeling like a small jolt through the dull numbing of the liquor.

I had never once in my life had a successful nap. If at any point during the day I ever somehow fell asleep, two things were guaranteed. One, I would wake up with a headache, and two, I would be sore as shit.

Drinking whiskey in a giant hot tub after skating twenty-seven laps in five minutes would have probably ensured both either way, but the nap really hammered it in.

My head was on her lap again, this time accompanied by a vague memory of me choosing it as my pillow an hour or so prior.

"Still drunk?" she asked, thumbing through her phone above me.

I slowly lifted, a pounding in my brain forcing me to press my fingers to my temple for relief. I was dehydrated and slightly hungover from day-drinking, but no longer inebriated.

I shook my head.

"Good. I think you were right yesterday; I don't think you should stay here." Her tone was flat, the same tone she'd taken with Nadine before.

"What?" I shrank, my voice an echo of itself.

"I'm trying to respect you when you tell me who you

are, but honestly, *I've* never been this confused before, and I'm starting to wonder if you aren't as sure as you think. If that's the case, I can't be your exploration phase, I can't fall for you just for you to change your mind and leave."

Her words were more than I could process, and I played them on repeat in my head multiple times before I'd even opened my mouth to conjure a response.

"I-I," was all I could manage.

"What are you doing here? What are *we* doing here?" she asked, but I didn't have the answer. I didn't even know myself.

I shook my head.

"Nia, look at me." She wasn't angry, but there was so much frustration in her tone that I couldn't bear to do it, couldn't devastate her expectations any further.

"We're friends," I answered, the only way I could sum up what little of this made sense to me.

"You do this shit with all your friends?" She tilted her head to the side, waiting for my answer.

"Well, no." I swallowed, uncomfortable with the only place every single question was leading.

"I asked you if you wanted to go with the others, with *friends,* and you came with me. Why did you come with me?" Her gaze never left mine, and it only made me itchier and itchier, burning from avoiding the truth.

"Aren't you my friend too?" I deflected with a question of my own, wondering if she'd already forgotten she'd agreed to be my friend, even after realizing I wasn't into girls.

"Why did you come with me, Nia?" She ignored me, ready for the answers on her own terms.

"Because I want to be around you," I whispered.

"Why do you want to be around me?" Her tone was annoyed, and it triggered every insecurity inside me that pushed me to lie and split the ridge between us even farther.

"You're right. I shouldn't be here." I agreed in a heavy panic, turning back into her room to grab the suitcase, and whatever I could manage to identify as mine in the process.

She was saying something, but I couldn't hear it anymore, could only focus on my own thoughts, castigating and shattering whatever was left of my confidence in half.

Tears fell freely; I had pulled the wrong piece and every *Jenga* block had come tumbling down. There was nothing left of me, nothing to salvage, nothing to build from anymore.

I pulled up the ride-share app, fighting my tear-filled vision and flickering through the fastest options. One leg in front of the other, I moved to get as far away from the apartment as I could at record speed. I settled on a driver who was four minutes away, but my card bounced, not even giving me the decency of stealing this one thing in my life.

"Agh!" I screamed out in frustration, throwing my phone on the snow-covered ground in front of me.

I couldn't stop crying now. I was pathetic, covered in day-old Midwest brown sludge-snow and crying outside somebody else's home.

"Hey!" Harvey's voice reached me from behind, as if it hadn't been the first time she'd yelled for me, and I turned my head slowly to find her still at her door, watching me from a distance. "Is it that hard to be honest with yourself?" She didn't lower her voice, a slight bitterness to her tone.

I didn't answer, didn't move.

"Just ask for help, Nia," she offered again, knowing there was nothing I could give in return.

Again, I didn't speak, didn't move, not until every part of me had finished breaking and my resolve had died. I was good at self-destruction. It was my best quality, actually. I could come together and break apart, then reinvent myself until the old Antônia would be so unrecognizable, I'd have no choice but to create an entirely new name for myself again.

I had come to Devil Town for closure, and there was officially nothing left for me here anymore.

I turned my head forward and grabbed my suitcase, walking through the sleet-covered grass and picking up my phone before finding my way to the sidewalk. It was twenty minutes to Skateland on foot.

I'd survived worse.

I was maybe a mile from Skateland when a car slowed down behind me, coming to a glacial roll at my side. Too embarrassed to look in their direction, I kept walking, my suitcase dragging behind me on wheels that bumped through the asphalt.

A honk blared, abrasive and impossible to ignore, forcing my head to turn to the left, where Jackie sat in the passenger seat, apparently drunker than before and hanging halfway out the window as she attempted to break through my dissociation. Ash was sprawled across the backseat with her feet dangling past the middle console, singing along with whatever song was playing on the radio.

I looked past them to see Mo in the driver's seat, a less-than-happy scowl painted over their face at playing chauffeur. "Get in, loser, we're going scrimmaging," Jackie howled, unable to contain her laughter.

I felt like shit, physically, mentally, and however else this misery could embody itself in me. I had never been so unhappy, yet so numb in my entire life. Everything felt wrong, and I couldn't even make sense of why.

I looked ahead again and continued to roll my suitcase forward.

"What's wrong with her?" Mo asked, but I tuned out the response, one foot in front of the other.

The car door slammed, and suddenly, I was being picked up and put in the backseat, where Ash rubbed her hands up and down my arms, as if to thaw me out. "She's fucking freezing. Blast the heat," she demanded, the concern in her voice making me wonder if I just couldn't feel it.

I hadn't put on a coat before leaving.

"Hey, Nia." Fingers snapped in front of my face.

I blinked.

"Nia!" More snapping.

"She's, like, catatonic." Mo's voice was serious, full of concern.

"I'm fine," I lied, leaning back into the seat.

The heat was suffocating now, drying my eyes out and burning my frostbitten fingers. "Can I have some water?" I rasped, dehydrated from day-drinking.

A bottle found its way between my hands, but I couldn't squeeze it, couldn't bend my cold fingers, and instead spilled it over my lap and the backseat of the car.

There was no nausea, no leaping of my stomach. There was nothing, just a vast emptiness inside me I could no longer stuff full of my own lies. I slowly moved, my bones cold and aching as I reached into my pocket to examine the phone. There was another crack on the screen, this one more like a chip.

I dug my nail into it, spreading the shards around the flat of my thumb in a soothing circular pattern until they'd effectively burrowed themselves into my skin. I took a deep breath, accepting defeat and sending the text.

I NEED A FLIGHT TO NEW YORK.

I turned the phone off. I wasn't ready for a conversation, not at this moment.

Selfish on my part, to demand the solution without the berating or the lectures. It was a disruption of the balance and natural order of things, but I didn't care anymore. I found I didn't care about anything.

Mo parked directly in front of Skateland's door before turning the engine off and staring back at me. "Are you good?"

"No," I answered, too honest and no longer caring to pretend anymore.

"Are you coming to practice?" Ash asked softly.

I turned to look in her direction, replaying her question once more in my head. "I don't know." I shrugged.

"What happened?" Jackie didn't bother to tiptoe around me.

"I did."

"Come skate," Jackie pleaded, the real reason any of them had given a damn about me.

I shook my head, "You don't need me to win." It wasn't a lie, but it hurt every part of my being to say it.

Half of me was tied up in a chair in my mind, locked behind the back porch of my consciousness, screaming for the imposter to remove their Antônia costume and let me take the wheel again. I couldn't let this be my end. I couldn't just ruin everything we'd worked for.

The other half of me knew I was both versions of myself, and that the dead and numb version of me was the only one who could finish what we started. Through was the only way out.

"You promised," Ash whispered.

"No. I didn't," I corrected, not a drop of emotion left in me.

"Did Harvey do something?" Mo asked. "She asked us to pick you up."

"No." Every part of me wanted to blame her, but all of this was on me. All of it was my mess, my problems, my issues, and for once in my goddamn life, it was time to own it.

"You'll feel better after you skate. Please?" Jackie begged.

I didn't answer, but they sat there, all three heads turned my way as they waited for my decision.

The door next to me opened from the outside, the chill of the winter air biting at my skin and waking me back up.

I had been outside in that for how long?

"Let's scrimmage, bitches," Nadine stood there, one hand on the door and the other holding her bag. "I'm dyin' to kick your ass." She turned her face my way and smirked, extending her hand in my direction.

Well, how could I say no to *that*?

Harvey hadn't showed up for warmups, probably a blessing in disguise, since my nerves were shot to hell. Even though Nadine was being disgustingly nice to me, all my hackles were raised. I was a mess.

Nadine had apologized for her outburst, but there was nothing to forgive. Whatever had happened was clearly between the two of them and had nothing to do with me, but I still thanked her. I appreciated the gesture, and the turn of a new leaf felt better than being afraid of running into her.

Besides, I was too busy contemplating someone else.

I'd done well at keeping my mouth from betraying me, only *thinking* it at least six times when the passing thought of *is she even going to show up?* played through my brain. Seventh time was the charm, and I might as well have summoned her.

Harvey arrived just as we were getting into our places on the track.

She really knew how to collect the attention of the entire room when she stormed in, throwing her shit haphazardly across the floor. She was already geared up, aside from her hands, which she quickly remedied, biting on her wrist guards one by one. She fished her mouth guard out of her pocket and slipped it in, the drastic cut of her jaw from the dental protection only making her look angrier.

As she slid her skates side to side, everyone on the track

waited for her to get into position as Mo threw the pivot panty straight into her hand. She wrapped the stripe over her helmet and got in the blocker line, ahead of me. Mo glanced between the two of us, once, not satisfied the second time, and on the third, they threw the yellow vest into Harvey's hand, putting her directly against me for this scrimmage.

Great.

I didn't even want to be here, and now, I was literally going to be chased by the person I was running from.

No, that wasn't true.

I was running from myself.

Mo blew the whistle, and with quick, easy strides, I was ahead of Nadine, crossing one foot over the other while staying aware of the blockers near me. I heard skates to my left, and just as I turned my head in that direction, I felt the hit on my right. My center of balance wasn't low enough, her hip catching me mid-rise and sending me sliding off the track on my knee pads.

She didn't even glance my way, didn't acknowledge the hit or celebrate it. Harvey just got back in the pack and finished the lap out, Nadine calling the jam and taking the win after lapping all the blockers.

I was still on the ground, paralyzed by something resembling shock.

The whistle went again, and Mo shouted something about me being chicken waste. Maybe I'd heard them wrong. Nadine circled me, extending her hand to help me up with a sympathetic smile on her face. We rounded back to the blue line together, getting into position for the next jam.

"Get up a little faster next time, Nia. The jam isn't over just because you took a hit," Mo chastised, but I knew that. Even a skater knocked down could still win a jam if their team's blockers could get the other jammer to the ground too. Speed could still determine the end result.

I knew all of that.

I just couldn't focus.

The whistle blew.

I dodged Nadine, learning her style faster than she could change it and taking the lead. One crossover after the other, and after I'd left the blockers just enough in the distance, I knew I'd have this one.

I didn't even see her coming for me. I only felt the hit of Harvey's shoulder knocking me to the side and shoving me toward the middle of the track, where Mo played zebra. I landed on my hip, a sharp pain shooting down the side of my leg, but I ignored it, bouncing back on my toe stops and finding my way into the pack.

I looked ahead to see Harvey grabbing Nadine's wrist and whipping her forward, sending her over the finish line and ending the jam.

I shook it off, skating the defeat away as I returned to position.

Stopped at the blue line again, Nadine and I were shoulder to shoulder, waiting for Mo's whistle to dictate the start of the next round. There was no delay after it, both of us skating in line as we moved the track under us. She used her hips to push me to the side, but I lowered my center of gravity, taking a deeper seat into my quad muscles.

My thighs burned, but my stance was solid; she would waste more energy trying to knock me down than trying to pass me. We were still closely matched in speed, but I felt certain this was the jam I'd take. I moved faster than before.

I made it through the opposing wall of blockers with the assistance of Mercy, filling me with hope that I'd actually take this win.

Nadine came from behind like someone had whipped her again, only she stopped directly in front of me, our chests colliding, giving Harvey just enough time to catch up and slam me outside of the boundaries of the track again.

I screamed in frustration. "What the fuck is your problem?" I knew the words weren't clear with my mouthguard in place, but I couldn't help it. It felt personal, even though I knew I was the only target for her on the track.

She chuckled, skating backwards past me, her hands in the air before pulling her mouth guard out. "I'm just blocking, princess."

Mo blew the whistle. "Nia, learn to take a hit, or you can't bout tomorrow."

What. The. Fuck?

"I think I can take a hit just fine," I grumbled, wiping the excess sweat from under my nose with the back of my arm.

It was blood.

Of course it was blood. Harvey hit like a fucking freight train, and yet somehow, I knew none of those slams had been what she was truly capable of. She was holding back, she was playing with me.

"Do you need a break?" Mo asked as all blockers on the track switched with those on the benches.

Harvey didn't sit. Instead, she swapped her stripe with

Nadine's star, handing the panty to Rae-volver, who was ready to pivot.

"No." I narrowed my eyes at Harvey, who looked more than happy to take the place of opposing jammer, next to me. My upper lip peeled up on instinct before the words flew out of my mouth. "Let's go, Kitty."

It was either the nickname or the shock of a tone she hadn't heard from me yet, but it was just enough to throw her off when the whistle went, giving me a few crossovers in advantage. I kept my corners tight, knowing just how to skate against Harvey to take the win. As long as I could keep her away from me, it was mine.

I pushed through the line of blockers without a hit and got in the front, ignoring all the outside noise until I'd lapped her and called off the jam.

I took the star panty off my head and threw it to the ground, not bothering to check in with the rest of the girls or stretch before skating to my cubby, my things nicely stacked inside.

I spit out my mouthguard, removing my helmet and then my wrist guards before sitting down and ripping the velcro off my skates. I could feel stares burning into me, but I was too angry to care, too bothered by everything around me to try to cool off. It was childish, and I felt it, but I was in my right to feel.

When you're a woman, your anger is either childish or irrational. It's never justified. So I didn't care to try to explain myself anymore.

I slipped my feet into my winter boots, not changing out of my sweat-drenched derby clothes before grabbing my phone from the duffel bag and turning it on.

There she was, waiting for me.

"Oi," I answered the call, pulling my hoodie over my head and pushing through the double doors.

It was frigid outside, colder than any other day since I'd gotten back to town. We had a running joke growing up here: Devil Town had two seasons, winter and construction. Days like today reminded me of grade school, wet hair turning into popsicles while I waited for the school bus outside of our apartment.

Back then, we only had one family car and my father used it for whatever odd jobs he could find without a working visa, anything to put food on the table while my mother's measly research school salary paid for our rent.

I didn't know we were poor then, and with rice and beans on the table every day, there was always something to be grateful for. We were too happy for me to think otherwise, but with age, the curtains fell, and the illusion dissolved. It wasn't until I turned fifteen and was shoved into the workforce that I realized how hard my parents had to work to create the magic that was my childhood.

"What?" I could feel the bite of her tone over the speaker, and I braced for the incoming lecture.

"I fucked up," I confessed, knowing the best way out of this was groveling and admitting my defeat.

"Eu não sei por que eu perco meu tempo com você. Tu não cresce, Antônia." Her tone was sharp, full of all the disdain she held for times like this.

When will I grow up? When will I stop wasting her time?

"I know. I'm sorry." I didn't bother with explanations; she only ever saw them as excuses anyway.

"Where is your car?" Her fingers clacked over a keyboard, as if she was multitasking on her laptop.

"It's totaled, and I just want to get home. Are you going to help me?" I should have waited for this call, but I wasn't in the mood to bow down and beg, and giving her this attitude would only lead to a catastrophic blowout.

"You skated." There was no emotion, excitement, or judgment in the two words, just her way of saying she knew me well.

"I did."

"And?" She was getting annoyed that I wouldn't dance the way she wanted me to.

I held my breath before answering, "And now I'm ready to go home."

"Is that so?" Harvey's voice had me whipping my head back in the direction of the doors, where she stood with my bag in her hand.

Shit.

"I'll call you back." I hung up, knowing the consequences were going to be severe.

"Don't hang up on my account. Just giving you the bag you left at my place." She dropped it next to me. "At least have the decency to tell *them*, yeah?" She glanced back toward the rink.

She got in her SUV, the engine starting, *Manchester Orchestra* playing obnoxiously loud, just the way she liked it.

If I had felt low before, I was now in hell.

The phone buzzed in my hands, my mother certainly reaching a new level of pissed off that even my ancestors could feel from beyond.

"Get your shit, skank. You're coming with me tonight," Nadine tossed casually over her shoulder, pulling car keys out of her pocket.

Jackie bounded behind her, giggling and grabbing my bag on the ground. I stood, and like a lost, homeless puppy, I followed.

"You're not driving." She side-eyed Jackie.

"It's my car!" Jackie argued.

"And you still reek of booze." She got in the driver's seat and closed the door behind her. "Get in, Nia."

Nadine had this overwhelming, commanding attitude to her that was equal parts nurturing and frightening. Her tone alone had me moving into action and getting into the passenger side of Jackie's car without question.

The two of them argued over the music the entire ride, never once settling on a song long enough to let it play to completion. Eventually, the music was drowned out by their arguing, something with absolutely no substance that I kept trying to tune out, but they were just too damn loud to ignore.

"I would have come, though!" Nadine's yell came out as more of a whine, and that was when I realized she was upset about not being invited to Freyer's today.

"You were acting kind of off, though, babe." Jackie teased, and they went back and forth a bit longer, each time yelling over one another until Nadine parked the car in front of the apartment.

I barely recognized it from the first time Harvey brought me here, after the accident. Nadine slammed her car door shut and marched to the door, Jackie following after in a frantic rush. I slowly made my way out, slinging all my bags over my shoulder and pulling my suitcase behind me through the open door.

"Guys?" I called out, but another door slammed.

Their shouting got progressively louder, something banged into a wall, and then quiet.

"Nadine?" I called into the apartment, closing the door behind me. "Jackie?" I sang out.

And then the moaning came, too clear and obvious to ignore, and I was now stuck inside a seven hundred square foot apartment listening to them have make-up sex. I scanned the room for the tv remote, putting on the first thing my thumb could click on and turning it up.

I was on my second episode of some show where they made everything into cake when they came out of the bedroom.

Nadine shamelessly wiped the bottom of Jackie's lip with her thumb before giving her a kiss.

Jackie giggled and then hopped onto the couch, damn near sitting on my lap as she burrowed into the rat's nest I had made for myself. "Make us popcorn?" she called out to Nadine, sticking her bottom lip out in a pout.

"Do you want real food, Nia? Jackie literally only snacks," she explained, walking toward the microwave with the popcorn bag already in hand.

"I'm okay." I shook my head, but my stomach grumbled in response, calling out my lie.

"Make us chicken nuggets too," Jackie added, giving me a wink.

Almost as if she knew me already. I eyed her suspiciously, her resolve breaking as she huffed with amusement. "What?"

"Nothing." I responded, the air of suspicion not discreet in my tone.

"Harvey said you're stubborn, that you need taking care of." Jackie grabbed the remote off my lap and thumbed through the movie options, flipping through a few times before giving up and staying on the cake show.

My jaw went slack, my brain unable to conjure a response to that statement. I didn't even know what I *could* say. Here Harvey was, pissing me off, making me feel and think things I didn't need to add to my pile of problems. Worse was that she was somehow *still* trying to take care of me when she wasn't even here.

And why did that make me so angry?

"I wish she'd mind her own business," I gritted, slightly

annoyed that everyone on this team now knew just how fucked I was in every aspect of my life.

Nadine snickered, dropping a bowl of popcorn into Jackie's lap before she rounded back to the kitchen.

"She would be doing it even if she didn't want to get into your pants. She can't help it," Jackie explained. "I don't even know why you're fighting it so much."

"What?" I turned my head in her direction. "I'm not gay!"

Nadine laughed, this time loudly. "And how many times have you said *that* this week?"

I frowned. "I'm not."

"Okay, so when you watch porn, are you looking at the guy or the girl?" Jackie threw a handful of popcorn into her mouth, waiting for my response.

"The girl, but that's not even relative. Nobody's looking at the men and all their dangly weird parts," I countered. "That doesn't make me gay."

Jackie laughed, all teeth and mouth wide open. "That's the gayest fucking thing I've ever heard, Nia."

"Stop saying gay," Nadine criticized from the kitchen. "L-l-l-lesbian." She flicked her tongue out at us. "Bean licker, carpet muncher, ssssapphic." She hissed the last one as she sat between us on the couch, a plate of air-fried chicken nuggets in her hand.

"You look pale, Nia." Jackie failed at biting back the joy on her face. "I can't believe you're having your coming out moment with us, right now." She squealed. "This is magical."

"I'm not!" I countered, but my brain was empty, as if it wouldn't allow me to seek refuge inside of my own mind.

Except for Harvey. She was running fucking marathons through my head, and it was endless torture to deal with. This stupid girl who invaded my life and treated me better than anyone ever had, who thought she had the right to make my problems her own, who made me laugh way too easily, who knew just how to push my buttons in order to force me to be a better version of myself.

My head felt bubbly, like there was no oxygen left in my body to nourish me.

This was hate.

This was loathing, this was fucking...

Love.

"Breathe," Nadine commanded.

I sucked a lungful of air through my mouth, the light-headed feeling easing some.

I groaned, dropping my back to the couch and wishing it would swallow me whole.

"Let's get high." Jackie's mouth stretched from ear to ear into a mischievous grin.

"You really *are* a bad influence." I mused, knowing I wouldn't turn down the only thing that would get me to crawl out of my head for once.

She pulled the pre-rolled joint out from a little plastic tube as Nadine walked over to the kitchen window, opening it all the way before grabbing a little glass ashtray from the table. Jackie flicked the lighter, taking a long drag and then another before exhaling. She passed it my way.

I didn't seek it out anymore, but I never turned down an opportunity to drink or smoke. It was a happy medium I had found that didn't trigger the addictive personality I knew I was capable of stoking, while also nurturing the little bit of me that craved spontaneity. I took a drag, holding it in and coughing a few times before taking a second hit of the joint.

It was exactly like Harvey said: sometimes, everything was all too much, and something to dull that sharp sting of existence didn't feel so bad every now and then.

By the second or the third time the little preroll made its way to me, I was stoned, my eyes the color of spider lilies and my eyelids heavy on my face. We were laughing about something on the cake show when I had finally gotten the courage to ask. "How did you know you were gay?"

Nadine perked up, like this was one of her favorite questions. "France," she said with a whimsical quality to her voice. "I was doing a summer exchange program. I was seventeen." She sighed. "Her name was Madeline."

"Like the children's cartoon?" Jackie snorted; Nadine shoved her away.

"She was my exchange family's daughter. She was so... free. Sexuality wasn't even a thing for her; she just *was.* Boys, girls, it didn't matter, Madeline just *loved*, you know?" She had the kind of look in her eye that almost made it seem like she was still in love, but then she turned toward Jackie, and the look intensified.

"And you knew because..." I needed more.

"I was addicted to her. I needed to be around her every second of the day, and when I wasn't, I was either thinking about her or asking someone about her." She smiled at the memory. "I thought I was going fucking insane."

Shit.

"And what about you?" I looked over at Jackie, who shrugged.

"I dunno. Harvey?" She snorted, shoving another

handful of popcorn into her mouth, not giving me any more explanation than that.

I honestly didn't need it.

Another episode of fake cake, and the two of them had disappeared back into the room, leaving me to stew, to boil myself alive in the brain soup of my mind until I was so uncomfortable, I had no choice but to give in, to turn my phone back on.

I hit ignore on the incoming call from my mother and sent a text instead.

HI

The chicken nuggets threatened their way up my throat, the three dots on the side of the phone indicating that a response was coming.

And then they were gone.

CAN YOU COME GET ME?

I took the biggest breath of my life, hating myself more than ever before. I didn't wait; I sent another.

PLEASE?

And then I turned the phone off, too afraid of rejection, too afraid of the words she had said earlier.

I can't be your exploration moment.

I was nodding off, still high from the weed, when headlights flashed into the window of Nadine's apartment. They blinked off and on a few more times before I realized what they meant.

My heart leapt, and I began to sweat. Suddenly, the expectations became heavier than I could bear, and every step toward that door grew more difficult. She was already waiting outside the car when I came through the door. Stepping toward me, she took each bag from my hand and threw them in the trunk.

There was no music.

For the entirety of the ride, there was nothing but dead silence, and me, too much of a coward to be the one to break it.

It was only when she'd closed the apartment door behind her, once she'd left my bags in the living room and began to walk away, that I could force my mouth open, like maybe I could say something, anything, to keep her from walking away.

"I didn't get a ticket home yet." *Why did I say that?* Why did that feel like the only thing I *could* say?

She turned slowly, hands in her pockets, eyes burning into my soul. "What are you doing back here?"

All I needed was an ounce of courage. I never backed down from anything in my life; I wasn't going to start now. "I wanted to be around you."

The hard look on her face softened, a smirk making its way there instead as she took a step toward me. "Yeah?"

I nodded.

"Why?" She narrowed her eyes at me, a hint of amusement on her face at the sight of me squirming.

"Because I can't stop thinking about you," I blurted out, my words as shaky as my hands.

"And?" She moved closer.

All the air in the room was gone. I was suffocating from keeping the truth bottled up inside me.

"And apparently, that means you might love someone. Or hate them." I shrugged. "Still out for debate." I took a step this time, closing the remaining distance between us.

"Please tell me I can kiss you." Her eyes were glued to my lips, and my stomach fluttered something awful.

"I think I'll die if you don't."

CHAPTER 21

PASSING THE STAR

I didn't know what I expected kissing Cat Harvey would be like, but it was clarity. It was as if I'd been consumed, devoured whole, then reassembled, like being spaghettified through a black hole and then recomposed on the other side. She held my face in her hands, the right one sliding past my ear and gripping the side of my head that still had hair. With her other thumb, she grazed the edge of my jaw, lifting my chin, giving her better access to my mouth.

Butterflies were having an entire fucking rager in my stomach. Every part of me was nervous, and my legs barely held strong beneath me. And then, she parted my lips with her tongue, and my throat let out a noise I'd been holding on to—too involuntary, but full of everything I still didn't know how to say.

As she cradled my throat in her hand, her thumb still at my jaw, I felt whole, held, surrendering to a kiss that was rearranging the entire fabric of my being, a kiss that would be changing every single one of my plans.

Before my tongue even tangled through hers, I knew I was irrevocably in love with her. I knew all I needed was to be loved back by her.

"Don't cry, Nia." Her chuckle was low as she broke free from my lips, wiping my cheek with the back of her fingers.

"I'm already brown and autistic. I wasn't prepared to add 'lesbian' to the mix." I threw the joke out too casually, making her uncomfortable. "You can laugh." Jokes about adding something to my ever-growing list of marginalizations and intersectionalities were the only way to manage. If I couldn't laugh, I would certainly cry.

"You called your mom today." Not a question; she *was* there for it, after all.

"I do that. When I've lost hope. I always deflect to her. It's the fucking *worst*," I groaned, her hands now at my waist, practically holding me up.

"Is it actually the worst to have a parent who will bail you out of anything at any time?" She wasn't trying to defend my mom; she was just trying to make sense of what she could see.

And I was turning into putty in her hands, melting into her touch.

"No. Only when she's keeping track of what I owe," I explained.

"Ouch." She cringed, dropping to the couch and pulling me with her.

She smelled so fucking good, like apricots and citrus and something else intoxicatingly sweet. It reminded me how filthy I still was, unshowered and in dirty clothes. I got off her lap with a bounce. "I need to shower," I declared, awkward as always.

She didn't disagree, walking ahead of me and opening a hallway closet, where she pulled out two folded towels and handed them to me.

The shower offered time to think that I did not need to grant my brain. I was too self-critical and hyper-analytical to have anything good come from being lost in my mind. I practiced three entire speeches to my mother, one for each conversation we still needed to have.

The one where I was done relying on her to exist.

The one where I admitted to being who I was.

And the one where I told her I was staying in Devil Town.

For good.

My legs were overcooked noodles under me, incapable of holding me up any longer as exhaustion set its way into my bones. Turning the water off and reaching for a towel to wrap me up, I dried off as best as I could manage before zombie-walking across the hallway and crash landing on her properly made bed.

"Let me see your hip." She nudged me before I could surrender to sleep.

I groaned, swatting her away.

"Let me see your hip, Nia." Her voice became stern.

Without opening my eyes, I raised the towel over the side of my leg, where my hip slammed into the track from one of her hits.

Her breath hitched. I didn't need to look down to know it was bad.

"Shit," she whispered.

"I bruise easily," I reassured her,

It wasn't a lie, and she didn't need to feel guilty about a scrimmage.

"Yeah, except now, you're gonna skate tomorrow trying to avoid falling on that side again. Skating hurt is how you get *more* hurt." She wasn't wrong. "Let me at least put something on it."

"It's fine," I grumbled, but I felt her weight lifting from the bed. Just a few moments later, she returned, her warm fingers sticky with a balm she circled against the tender skin. "You can keep doing that," I hummed, letting sleep win.

I woke up in Harvey's arms, towel still firmly around my body, but the blanket covered both of us. I didn't think people actually slept like this, twisted and tangled into each other, and yet here I was, the most rested I'd felt all week.

"I like you smelling like my soap." Her voice was groggy and full of sleep, right against my ear.

Every hair on my neck came to a stand once she took a big inhale, a satisfied hum falling from her lips. I turned, rotating with the towel until I'd come to face her, my hand on her heart and her chin above my head.

We stayed this way for a while, for more breaths than I could count, for far more scripts than I could rehearse through my brain.

"You're quiet. What are you thinking about?" she asked.

"Nothing," I admitted. "Everything." A nervous laugh bubbled out of me, and her fingers grazed my jaw line, lifting my gaze up to hers with a gentle tug. "It feels too good to be true."

Her expression softened, and she didn't hurry with her words. "It can feel like that when you're used to someone always pulling the rug out from under you." Her hand covered mine, like she was trying to press it even closer to her heart. "But I promise, as long as you're honest with me, I will keep that from ever happening. Do you trust me, Nia? Can you trust me enough to let go?"

I was locked in the vortex of her stare, finding that the only time I'd ever truly wished to be perceived was through her lenses. With a nod, I exhaled. "I can."

Somehow, it didn't feel like such a heavy promise.

"How did you know you were gay?" I asked, not quite done processing and needing to have this conversation just one more time.

"I've always been gay." She shrugged.

"What?" I laughed out, the concept quite literally foreign to me, "What does that even mean?"

"I didn't grow up with the heteronormal expectation. My uncle on my dad's side is gay, and my mom's sister paved the way for me. So, when I came home at the age of ten and said I had a girlfriend, no one batted an eye. That was it. I'd declared it, and there was never a conversation about it again." It was so casual coming out of her mouth.

"That sounds nice. Your family sounds great." I sighed exhaustedly, thinking of my own.

"It has its positives and negatives." She shook her head, squeezing me a little harder.

"Never having hid from yourself?" I asked, surprised she could feel regret toward something like that.

"Yeah, my family was always accepting, loving, and proud of me. But do you know what it's like being known as the resident lesbian in a tiny town? Teachers didn't have a clue what to do with me; they'd make me change clothes in the boys locker rooms after gym class. Every girl in Smithville thought I was attracted to them, so they didn't want to be my friend. It was lonely as hell. You're othered, and you don't even get a chance to prevent it, to try to—"

"Lie about who you are?" I asked.

"It doesn't matter. You wouldn't get it. You would have probably been just like the other girls, the ones who wouldn't even sit around me for fear of catching *the gay*, and yet, ten years later, they came crawling to my bed to discover themselves."

Hitting that nerve felt like cutting the wrong wire to a bomb.

"You think I'm just here to discover myself?" I couldn't hide the hurt in my voice. I understood why she felt the way she did, but that didn't mean I was like the others.

"That seems to be all I'm good for. I'm just tired of getting used, tired of being a steppingstone in everyone's path to discovery before they throw me away." She put on a mask of indifference and began to pull away from me.

"Why do you think I'm going to throw you away?" I wanted to be mad, offended, but how could I when she was flaying herself open for me, showing me the root of her scars?

Her face fell flat. "Isn't that why you keep ignoring your mom's calls? Because telling the truth would be too permanent?"

I froze. There were a million reasons why I wasn't

taking her calls, but Harvey was choosing to focus on this specific one.

She wasn't wrong. Calling my mother meant facing myself, and I wasn't sure I was ready for that yet.

"Harvey, wait." I grabbed her wrist, pulling back into her hold.

Her scowl carved deeper into her forehead.

"Are you afraid of what your parents will think?" she asked.

"I mean, yes, but also no. Mostly because I already know how they will react." I stared past her. "My mom will roll her eyes and assure my father that it's just a phase because she could never believe I know enough about myself to be this sure of anything. My dad will get uncomfortable, say some weird joke about how he would probably be a lesbian too if he was a woman."

"And in the long run, when you prove to them it's not a phase?" She was so close to my face, her body pressed up to mine.

"And we're sure it's not?" I tried to tease, but the intensity of her stare had me wanting to disappear under the sheets.

"Do I feel like a fucking phase, princess?" She held my chin between her thumb and forefinger, waiting for a response.

"No. You don't feel like a phase."

She was the only person I would ever want, the only one I needed.

"You don't have to do it now. You can take as long as you need to, but you have to talk to her eventually, Nia." Her tone was soft again, the gentlest it had ever been. "You can't stay in limbo forever."

"I know," I whispered, more for myself than her.

She smiled and then stole the breath out of my lungs with another kiss. This time, her hands traveled up and down my side, squeezing, tugging, feeling for any sign of life from me.

I pressed into her body, the desire to be as close as possible all consuming, dangerous, unquenchable. Squeezing my legs together to dull the burning need between them, I groaned into her mouth, her knee resting just below the apex of my thigh.

"All right!" She broke the kiss and leapt out of bed with a startling speed. "And you still owe me beans, so I figured we can go to the store, come back, do a little cooking before we head to Skateland for Slam Night. The Red Queens are bouting against The Five Skulls league before us. Lonnie likes us to all support each other, even if we're going to kick their ass eventually."

I stretched out, yawning and covering my head with the rest of the blanket to disappear. "I'm going back to bed."

"I'll give you five more minutes, and then I start blasting music," she threatened.

"So..." I start, with full intention to spark a match. "Tell me about this girlfriend you had who fed you feijoada?" I brought a hand to my chest, dramatizing my fake hurt.

Hiding my amusement, I stirred the pot of beans, taking just a bit of the broth into the spoon and blowing on it.

"Aw, baby, don't be jealous. Her beans didn't smell nearly as good as yours." She smiled that goofy crooked smile of hers, the one that looked so damn good on her face and no one else's.

She wrapped her arm around my waist from behind, her nose burying into the crook of my neck as I lifted the spoon. "Taste," I said, dropping the broth onto the base of my palm, the same way my grandmother would when teaching me to cook.

Her mouth lowered to my hand, her lips closing around the meaty part of my palm where she licked it clean, never once breaking eye contact with me. I bit back a smile, flattening my lips into a thin line as I closed my fingers, bringing my fist to my heart.

"Does it need salt?" I asked, knowing it didn't.

"No, it's perfect. When can I eat it?" She leaned her head over the pot.

I closed it, switching on the slow cooker and turning on the timer. I'd struggled with feeling enough my entire life. Brown enough, mixed enough, *Brazilian* enough. But here, in her kitchen, cooking a meal for someone I loved with nothing but joy in my heart, I felt the most connected to my people. I felt the reach of my grandmother span across time and space, holding my hand around that wooden spoon and connecting me to all my ancestors in an embrace that felt like home.

"In ten hours." I grinned at her feigned physical discomfort from being forced to wait. "It'll be perfect," I chirped. "We'll either eat in celebration or mourning, exactly what feijoada is for. Now we just kill some time." I grinned. "What should we do?"

She pushed me against the cabinet, her body flush with mine and her hands on either side of me, trapping me in. "I have an idea or two."

"W-wait," I stuttered, unsure why hesitation came more naturally.

"What? You've been shoving your tongue down my throat all morning. Is this too fast for you?" She took a step back, giving me the space she thought I needed.

"No, it's not that. It's just..." I couldn't put the words to it. I'd never hesitated when it came to sex with men, even if they couldn't get me off or if I wasn't into it. The expectation had never felt this high before. "Sex feels different somehow," I admitted.

"Are you nervous, princess?" She tilted her chin in curiosity.

"Of course I'm nervous!" I laughed out like a crazy person. "I'm disgustingly insecure, and I literally live inside my own head. You've been with tons of women." I tried explaining, but there was no clarity in her expression, no sort of understanding. "What if I don't measure up? What if I'm bad at going down on you?" My panic was increasing with each word. "What if I smell?"

She reached out for me, gripping my arms, holding me up, keeping me from falling. "Would these fears go away if I had a dick?"

I took a moment to think about it, unsure if my response would somehow be twisted into something that could offend her. "I mean, maybe? It's not like you're some pussy-obsessed guy who doesn't care what it looks, smells, or tastes like as long as you get to have it."

She laughed, hearty, obnoxiously teasing laughter that came straight from her chest. "Who said I'm *not* pussy obsessed?"

My cheeks heated, an attempt to hide my face behind my hands thwarted by her grip on my wrist. I playfully shoved at her shoulder, but she pulled me in tighter, our chests pressed together as I raised my chin up to look at her. She pulled a rogue strand of hair away from my face and tucked it behind my ear. "We go as slow or as fast as you want, Nia," she assured me before sealing the promise with a kiss, the kind I gave my whole body to.

I shook my head, every cell in my body wanting this moment to last, to turn into more. "I want this. I want you."

"Do you want to shower first?" she offered, like she could read my mind, but her hands traveled, moving under my shirt, her touch softer than ever.

She was weaving through my entire soul, and nothing about a shower was calling to me at this moment. Nothing about interrupting her felt right or reasonable.

"No," I breathed out, barely breaking from our kiss before continuing again.

In a few moves, she pushed me toward the back of the couch, lifting me slightly so I was sitting on it, finally at level with her. She pulled away, just enough to give me space to think, letting me back away again. I grabbed her wrist and pulled her into me, closing my legs around her waist.

"I'm going to devour you whole," she breathed into my ear, a pool of desire flooding my core.

"Fuck," I exhaled, barely surviving the intimacy of this moment alone and unsure how much more I could take.

Her hands slid down, stopping at the tops of my thighs where she squeezed.

It was painful without her mouth on me. Reaching for her again, I pressed my lips to hers, the same softness greeting me once more. Her thigh was between my legs, her hands still steadying me when a throaty noise escaped me.

She pushed my chest, throwing off my balance and forcing me to fall back into the cushions with a squeal as she walked around the couch.

"What gives?" I frowned.

"Undress." Her tone was no longer playful, laced in seduction and spilling with yearning.

For me.

She crashed down on the couch, legs spread out as she leaned back, and I came to a stand in front of her. I pulled the shirt over my head, no bra in place for the day yet. The urge to cover my chest was immense, but the look in her eyes begged otherwise, threatening beautiful violence with just a look. It was the kind that would bruise my soul and leave a permanent mark. I wasn't even wearing my own pants or underwear, just her clothes from last night. I lowered her boxers to the ground.

Her eyes scanned me, hunger, thirst, and bloody desperation all caught in that stare. Once her gaze met mine, the look in her face softened, a smile pulling at the corner of her mouth. "You're so beautiful, Antônia." She said the entirety of my name, and my heart caught on fire, a shakiness to her voice like she was nearly as nervous as I was.

But that couldn't be right. Not her. Nervous for me?

I'd never felt so awkward in my life, shy, almost virginal. I wasn't in any way shape or form, but somehow here, in front of her, I felt exposed. My first time had meant less, barely a memorable blip on my calendar, but here she was, somehow capable of turning this into an entire national holiday.

"Sit on my lap." She beckoned me with a slight tilt of her chin.

"On your lap?" I parroted her, biting my lip anxiously.

She nodded slowly.

One foot in front of the other, with breaths that stammered on every pull, I reached her. "Like this?" I asked, attempting to straddle her.

"No." She shook her head, first giving my body one final

appreciative look before gripping my hips with both her hands and turning me around. "Like this."

I fell into her hold, letting her guide me the rest of the way onto her lap. I was shaking with fucking nerves, forgetting to breathe, taking large gulps of air to compensate.

"Relax." Her voice was soft, her breath cool on the back of my neck as she brushed my hair to the side.

I didn't know the meaning of the word, but with her under me, it felt like she was holding the weight of my whole being—all my worries, all my fears, all my problems. I melted into her, letting her take the entirety of me onto her.

"Now tell me what you want from me, princess," Harvey whispered in my ear.

The most dangerous thing she'd asked of me yet.

"W-What I want from you?" I turned my head, green eyes meeting mine.

She nodded slowly, her gaze dropping to my mouth, where I still tortured the flesh under my teeth. Her thumb grazed over my bottom lip, rubbing back and forth until she freed it from my bite.

"I want the moon, the stars. I want an entire constellation made of us." I nodded, turning my head back to her and growing a spine, claiming exactly what my heart demanded for once in my life. "I want to feel you in my soul."

"Done," She breathed out.

Her mouth found mine, our tongues tangling, the feeling of any space between us shrinking to an unreal size. My hands stayed frozen on her thighs, paralyzed and afraid to move, afraid to do anything that could end this moment. She held no such reservation; her fingers moved through my hair while the other hand traveled down my side.

That same hand slowed at my belly, her thumb gently grazing my skin just below my breast. I was desperate to be touched, to feel her all over me, and yet all I could do was hold on to her, to wait for whatever she'd give me. "Please," I broke our kiss to whisper.

She smirked, a dark devious curl of her lip, as if she thrived on being in control. The hand stroking my hair stilled, then wrapped around thick strands and pulled, twisting my head to the side and eliciting a gasp from me. She took my exposed neck into her mouth, gently making her way to the spot where my neck and my collar met.

Kissing had never been so erotic, not with anyone else before. She had barely touched me, and I was a puddle on her.

"Spread your legs for me." The hand on my stomach moved south, and I obeyed, my heart hammering in anticipation for the feel of her fingers.

The whimper was autonomous, an involuntary response conjured by my throat and betrayed by my lips as her fingers grazed my center. Her touch was barely there, nearly non-existent, almost imaginary, forcing me to squirm desperately on her lap.

Her other hand softened its pull on my hair, skimming down my arm and then cupping my breast. I moaned, her thumb gently circling around the hard bead of my nipple.

"I can feel how wet you are through my pants." Her voice was a low hum now, every word turning me further from a puddle and into an ocean. "Wanna feel?"

I nodded, but I would have nodded for anything at that moment. Taking my hand under hers, she guided it down, where scorching heat and sticky fervor waited. I didn't think

I'd ever been this wet before, and knowing it was dripping all over her was equal parts enthralling and evoking.

She moved my fingers, sliding them through my folds, slick with desire, using my hand to rub the swollen bud of my clit. I cried out, reveling in pleasure with every stroke. Gripping my hand at the wrist, she lifted my fingers to her face, taking both into her mouth as she licked them clean.

Her tongue swirled around my fingers, and a deep need to clench my thighs followed, but she used her legs to keep them spread, her free hand slapping down on the sensitive skin of my inner thigh.

I moaned again, another soft plea falling from my lips as I turned into lava on her lap.

"Ask me just a little nicer, princess," she whispered softly.

"Please. Please, Kitty." I mumbled, drunk with lust and need for this woman who could turn me inside out with so much ease.

Her fingers dove inside me, rubbing exactly where and how I needed without error. Her thumb stayed on my clit, her middle and ring finger buried deep inside me, curling like a hook as she kept me firmly in her hold. She moved rhythmically, every jolt of her fingers conducting an orchestra, with me as the instruments.

Harvey's lip grazed my neck once more, and the hand on my thigh eventually moved, her entire arm hooking under my knee and lifting me back into her even further, deepening the reach of her fingers. I was fully exposed. I'd never felt more raw, more vulnerable in my entire life, but in her hold, I'd also never felt safer, more willing to let go.

I turned my head to her, our eyes never breaking from

each other as she moved her skillful fingers inside me until I fully unraveled, quaking and trembling around her in the strongest orgasm I'd ever felt.

"Fuck," I breathed out, leaning into her chest as she unwound her arm beneath me. Turning to face her, I stared at the smug look she wore so well. "I want to see you naked."

Her expression changed, a stunned look I'd yet to see on her face.

I gripped her shirt at the hem, and she pulled away from the couch, helping me lift it off her. She wasn't even naked yet, but Harvey in a sports bra, her hair hanging just over her eyes, the button on her pants undone, was art. Standing, she dropped her jeans to her ankles and stepped out of them. My courage was wavering with every second, but once the rest of her clothes came off, I knew for certain.

If I wasn't sure before, I was certainly a lesbian now.

The urge to touch her was the only thing running through my mind, the only thing dictating my movements, the only thing feeding any spark of electricity to my brain.

"I want you so much." She'd called me beautiful, but she was more. She was beyond that, and since there wasn't a word I could find to describe her, I decided my desire was enough. "Tell me what to do?" I asked awkwardly as she sat back on the couch.

She shook her head. "You got it." Her tone was teasing.

I shoved her toward the arm of the couch, forcing her to lay down and straddling over her. Skin on skin, the proof of what she could do to me still sliding down my thighs and now dripping over her bare belly, I lowered my mouth to hers once more.

I had never wanted to kiss someone so much before, never wanted to be swallowed up whole just be closer to them.

Any reservations left my body, and I slid down, her head on a pillow as she opened for me with a shaky breath. Asking her to tell me what to do now felt borderline comical. How could I *not* know what to do, staring face to face with the only thing that could truly make me believe in God? In magic?

Surreal in beauty.

Divine.

A hot breath escaped from my lips, a gasp of anticipation echoing from her throat before I lowered all the way, tasting her. Where I expected salty instead came a burst of sweetness on my tongue, her moans encouraging me further. I savored the moment, relishing her flavor in my mouth while my hands wanted nothing more than to explore every shape, every curve of her body beneath me.

My thighs squeezed, containing a newfound rush of pleasure in my core. The littlest gasp or high pitched noises I forced from her somehow working to throw me further off the edge. Getting her off was the hottest thing I'd ever experienced, and having her fold under me was now my greatest accomplishment.

My right hand explored south, victory surging through my mind as my fingers dug their way inside her, nothing but slick arousal waiting for me. Another moan, this one louder, and one finger, then another, found its way inside her, my mouth still firmly stationed on her clit.

I mimicked her movements, reaching up and feeling the same ridged spot she used to trigger my orgasm. Another cry from her lips, this time higher than before as she squirmed under me.

I broke free only to laugh, a feeling of satisfaction washing over me as I held her legs in place with my arms and dove back in. She bucked, her hips arching with every pull of her orgasm as her hands firmly entwined in my hair. She tugged, gripping tight, holding on to me until her body had calmed from each wave of pleasure.

I came up, wiping my mouth with the back of my hand before crawling on top of her. She turned to the side, pulling me in and holding me into her chest.

I'd never felt more whole.

W e were all nervous; every single one of us showed up early to get our feet under us. The only person missing was Lonnie, and a crater cracked open inside my chest in their absence.

I had just painted the number sixty-four on my arm with eyeliner. It was my registered number with the WFTDA. The same number I chose nearly a decade ago at eighteen. My mother's birth year. I'd moved on to running ladder drills on my toe stops, facing off against Nadine, when the first challenging team came through the doors. Their excitement was contagious, and that tingly feeling I only felt on Slam Nights returned. They packed their way into the locker room, and Mo blew the whistle to gather our attention.

The Devil's Dames league wasn't separated into an A or B team. Blockers drew straws to see who would be benched tonight, as every skater had met their eligibility requirements for bouting. Harvey stood to the side, no doubt guaranteed to be skating as pivot.

The benched players headed to Lonnie's place, where they'd be breaking out all the decorations and merch bins to sell during the bout. Mercy was among them, a slight letdown, since that meant she wouldn't have my back tonight.

But there was only room for four blockers and a jammer on the track from each team, and aside from a few prepared replacements, there was no need for extra players on the sideline when we could be raising money to keep the rink in place.

Mercy took to the t-shirt stand, hanging up every variation of Devil's Dames clothing to have ever existed since our inception. Nadine's little sister was already locked down, manning the popcorn stand like a little twelve-year-old boss. Two girls I hadn't officially been introduced to hung colored flags off the poles, and another turned on the blinking lights.

The second team came through the door, polite nods sent our way as they made a single file into the other locker room. The smell of buttery popcorn and sweet cotton candy filled the air, and before I'd even realized it, the announcers were setting up their tables to the side of the track.

I leaned into the partition wall, fighting off a slight wave of nausea triggered by the rush of anxiety. Harvey's hand covered mine, heavy, soft, and securing as she laced her fingers through mine.

"Are you okay?" She nudged me with her shoulder.

"I can't breathe," I confessed, struggling to take in any oxygen. "It feels like everything is ending tonight."

"Maybe that's because it is." Harvey shrugged.

"What?" The words sent a chill down my spine.

"Maybe everything has to end in order to start again."

The look on her face was so sincere, so full of truth.

All the words I needed to hear, and she was always there to deliver them.

"I think I need to call Lonnie. It doesn't feel right doing this without them," I admitted.

She nodded, and with a tilt of her head, she gestured toward Lonnie's office. Her fingers were still entwined in mine as she led me there, whistling to Mo so they'd evacuate the space for me. Mo stood from the chair behind Lonnie's desk, not bothering to ask as they tightened their ponytail before giving me the room.

"Want me to stay?" Harvey asked.

I shook my head. This was just for us.

Shutting the door behind me before skating over to the chair, I hit the video call button and set my phone on their desk, using some dirty coffee mug growing mold on the inside to prop it up.

They picked up on the first ring.

"Hey, brat." The camera shook as they searched for a place to rest it, settling on their mother's hospital tray and giving me a good look at the both of them.

Lonnie was squeezed in their mother's bed, cuddled up to her frail little body all hooked up to cords and tubes.

"Momma, it's Nia," they told her, the kind of softness in their voice that never came out anymore. "I told you she'd come back."

A rush of emotion swept over me, but I held back the tears. This moment wasn't about me; I had to stay strong.

"Hi Momma Green!" I sniffled back any sign of sadness.

"Nia, baby," she croaked, the smallest bit of light

returning to her. "I'm turning on channel two to watch you today." Her words shot straight into my heart like an arrow, the same exact words she had said to me five years ago, before the bout that changed everything.

She'd been cheering me on that day; perhaps she was stuck in that memory with me too, never truly freed from that moment. Lonnie looked worried, like I was going to break the spell of lucidity and correct her.

"I'll be skating my best for you, Momma." I winked, the tear rolling down, a free agent with a mind of its own.

Lonnie kissed their mother's head, grabbing the phone and standing. Neither of us said anything until they'd fully left the room and shut the door behind them.

"Are you okay?" I asked, knowing the answer and feeling stupid for asking anyway.

"She hasn't spoken in two weeks, Nia." Their confession didn't ease my pain. "But she spoke to you." Lonnie's eyes were filled with tears, and I could no longer hold back my own.

"I'm sorry, Lon." Not for death, not for their mother, not for this overwhelming grief. "For everything. You deserved better from me."

"Shut your mouth, you little shit. I love you. You needed to grow up to come back, and I'm proud of the woman you've become." They wiped their cheek with the back of their sleeve.

Those words meant more than anything. They were the words I was desperate to hear from my own mother, but here, right now, coming from Lonnie, they were everything, everything my mother could never give me, and I was somehow finally okay with that.

Maybe that was the first step to healing this crater in my chest.

I'd spent my entire life with the belief that family was blood, and no matter what, you couldn't break away, that friendships came and went, but nobody would be there for you like your own.

But these people had shown me that family meant so much more.

"I'm gonna kick their asses for you, okay?" I promised. "I'll see you when you come back."

"Count on it, twerp." Lonnie disconnected the call, and my heart felt lighter.

Things felt right.

The Red Queens were already on the track when I exited the office, the announcer calling out each skater from the Five Skulls league as they made their entrances. The Skulls wore something that looked like fake armor over their protective gear, as if they were ready for battle. Their dedication was thrilling, reminding me exactly why I loved this fucking sport, and making me glad we weren't up against them tonight.

Just as I gave my mental graces, the double doors swung open, the West Town Dollies' pivot charging through first. She was probably six feet tall without skates, and my knees hurt just at the thought of taking a hit from her tonight. The back of her shirt said Death-Stroker, her hair in pigtails hanging high above her head.

Their colors were red and white, and with the way they'd coordinated, they looked like Harlequin dolls.

Half those skaters were giants, and I was doubly afraid to see what their jammer looked like. I felt a tug on my hand again, Harvey's presence easily centering me and pulling me from the quicksand of my own mind. She tilted her head, gesturing me to where the rest of our team sat, ready to watch the other two leagues go head-to-head.

"You never told me what the beans thing meant," she whispered, her words hot in my ear from proximity in an attempt to beat the volume of the crowd.

I stumbled over my skates, unprepared to give her an answer.

"Tell me." She nudged me, pulling me under her arm and squeezing my waist.

"Eating beans." I bit back a laugh trying to get it out coherently. "It's another way Brazilians say eating ass."

The expression on her face was worth capturing—too bad I didn't have my phone handy, because I would have framed and hung the photo for the rest of our lives.

"And you've just been letting me casually toss this in conversation all week?" She laughed in disbelief.

"Absolutely." I threw her a grin, turning my attention to the rest of our teammates.

It was packed, and by the time the starting whistle went off, there was barely space to move, and Mercy's booth had already sold out of shirts and hoodies. Nadine's little sister was being worked overtime in concession, and another skater had joined to help move things along.

This place was alive.

It was the home I remembered, and every minute here felt like a jolt of the defibrillator, bringing me back to my body.

Despite their outfits, the Red Queens took down The Skulls with ease, their jammer impossibly fast and skilled on their feet. I was nowhere near ready for that kind of speed, but thankfully, I didn't have to be.

I turned back to our skaters, each one glowing with the kind of confidence that only filled me with excitement. Nadine stretched in a dancer pose, holding her skate and bringing her foot damn near her head. I had no idea how she could manage to stay upright on solely four wheels while maneuvering that kind of shape, but I was impressed.

We'd be jamming together tonight; not against each other, but in support. She threw a giant grin my way that I instinctively returned, and then she fell into me, cursing Rae-volver, who had thrown her off balance as a prank. Ash sat on a bench, her knees bouncing anxiously while her eyes stayed glued to the track, her focus on one thing and one thing only.

Winning.

The skaters emptied the track, and the lights turned down, nothing but the soft glow of floor lighting left for guidance. My palms were drenched in sweat, and acid rose up my throat. "Guys, I don't think I can do this," I confessed, the words making their way out of my mouth before I had given them permission to do so.

"You're okay. You're great. You've got this." Harvey was there, in my ear, doing her best to keep me from chickening out.

All their voices joined together, fear, persuasion, and everything in between trying to urge me to stay the course. I couldn't make out a word they were saying, and then the spotlight came on in the middle of the track.

"Slam Night is only Slam Night if the Devils come out!" the announcer hyped up the crowd. "Give it up for

Mad Morgan!" Mo flew out onto the track, donning their Mad Morgan shirt with the word *coach* in big, bold font underneath.

We would be seriously missing Lonnie's direction tonight, but I trusted Mo's leadership and dedication to our team just the same. The announcer called the zebras next, and two skaters in striped shirts made their way to the center of the rink, taking their place as referees.

One by one, he announced us, reciting each skater's tag line with more and more excitement until the crowd was ready to burst. "Gotham City's finest villain, let's hear it for Harvey Dent-her-face!" Harvey blew me a kiss, skating backwards into the track and waving to the audience as she took her place behind the pivot line.

"Wait, I didn't give him my tag line!" I remembered, panicking, finding any reason possible to back out.

Nadine laughed, holding my shoulders in place, giving me nowhere to go but the track.

And then, I heard the words I hadn't heard in five years.

"She's hell on wheels, and she doesn't quit. Make some noise for Nia-Death-Experience." Every sound came to a muted hush, like the inside of a seashell. All I could hear was a muffled symphony of reverberations.

My feet moved beneath me on command, though my mind clung desperately to consciousness, the threat of blacking out right here, right now, far too real. I took position behind the jammer line, the announcer calling for Nadine, who skated straight to the bench where the reserve skaters would be waiting for a trade-out.

And then, it was the Dollies' turn.

T he whistle was loud in my ear. "False start," the zebra called out, gesturing to my foot over the line.

I clenched down on my mouthguard, internally cursing myself for stupidly causing the penalty and yielding my position at the signal for the jam to start. I shoved through the pack until I could feel Harvey's hands on my hips, ensuring Death-Stroker couldn't get to me. With a supportive shove, I was free, ahead of the blockers and leagues in front of the Dollies' jammer.

I was through the line with ease, calling the jam off once I'd gotten far enough ahead that there was no way she could pass me.

All nerves had officially vacated my body, and I proudly reclaimed every ounce of confidence. Waiting for the next whistle, I hopped from side to side on my skates as the blockers from both teams got in their spots ahead of us. Malice in Wonderland was the jammer to my side, and judging by the look on her face, she was not happy about the way the last jam ended. We went four more times, the next round easily hers, but the following three were no contest against me.

Half-time was nothing but anticipation, drowning in sweat and water that Mercy deliberately drenched us with to cool down. No time to talk, no time for discussion, only a strategic plan Lonnie had practiced with Mo to deliver to us tonight.

And deliver we would.

I was back in the line for the second half next to their jammer, shoulder to shoulder, no shred of good-sportage left between us. We pushed against each other, waiting for the whistle to move through the starting line.

Just like that, she pulled back, nearly throwing me off balance, falling toward her as the skaters moved. Righting my stance, I shoved back, hitting her with a hip check before reaching for Ash's hand hanging behind her. With a whip of her shoulder, I was through again, skating clean ahead of the blockers while my team protected me.

Before I could hit the line, a slam on my bruised hip threw me across the track. The pain exploded through me, and instinctively, I jerked my body to the side, falling on my ass to protect my already battered and bruised hip.

"Fuck!" I shouted through my mouth guard, coming to my toe stops, but not fast enough to stop Malice from taking the lead.

I moved the track beneath my feet, skating like my life depended on it while I worked to catch up. Then, they were behind me, both Jackie and The Vominatrix, as they coordinated a well-timed shove to push me to the front. It was enough, and just when Malice thought she had the win, I came out ahead, stealing the jam from her.

There was barely time to celebrate, but the moment I moved to my place, I felt the tug of Mo's hand against my wrist. "Take a bench. You almost broke your leg again out there trying to avoid that fall."

I wanted to argue, wanted to shout and fight and tell them I was good, I was great. I could give us this win.

Then, I looked at Nadine, strapping on her wrist guards as she stood from the bench, eager for her own chance. For the first time in my life, I wanted to give someone else that chance, that moment of glory. It wasn't meant to be just mine; it was meant to be ours, and I knew with every fiber of my being that she was capable of it too.

"Get 'em, killer." I grinned at her, placing my hand on her shoulder. "She's weak on her left foot."

She nodded, slipping her mouthguard in and taking her place behind the line.

I didn't need to destroy myself over a victory, didn't need to be self-sacrificing or get hurt in order to be a winner. In order to be *their* hero. I could be my own damn hero, and that meant sometimes letting someone else do the saving.

Nadine was a powerhouse against Death-Stroker, solid enough to bounce all her checks, to remain unaffected by them as she skated through two more wins. Their coach turned red, furious about the defeat, laying into them before subbing them and their jammer out with a much greener-looking skater.

Her skates were shiny, wheels too clean to have gotten much use, and I wondered if her skates were even broken-in enough to skate comfortably. Unlikely. She looked awkward making her way to the jammer line, where she anxiously smiled up at Nadine.

This was going to be easy.

I leaned back onto the wall, crossing my arms and preparing for the slaughter, for the feel of a victory again. There was nothing that felt as good as winning.

Except Harvey under me.

It felt like a burning in my veins, the feeling of being watched. The more I tried to ignore it, the more it beckoned me, like the pull of a current. My stomach churned, uncomfortable with the feeling, and I stood, distracted from the bout.

She was there.

In an ivory and blue pants-suit combo, her hair wrapped up in a bun, my mother stood behind the partition, her eyes fixed in my direction.

It was impossible to stay focused on the bout, the entire second half moving in a blurry haze, dissociation taking over and only letting me perceive enough to notice our win. Our stare-off never once broke, attention solely on each other for every agonizing minute that now moved slower than ever before.

I was being lifted off the ground by multiple arms, the sudden movement jerking my attention away from my mother, to Nadine, who reached for me, also six feet in the air. I interlaced my fingers through hers and lifted our fists up high, screaming and cheering bloody victory.

Once my skates touched the ground, I turned to Harvey, our lips locking as I fell hard into her embrace. "I knew you could do it," she whispered in my ear.

But this wasn't over. My biggest dragon stood, unconquered, waiting to breathe down fire on everything that now mattered to me. Harvey caught the way my gaze drifted, finding the point of focus and squeezing my hand tight.

"Is that her?" she asked, not even an ounce of surprise in her voice that my mother would be here.

I nodded, swallowing a hard gulp. "I guess let's do this." I pulled her with me.

"You want me there?" she asked, hesitant for the first time since I'd met her.

"I *need* you there," I confessed, the only thing I knew for sure.

We were six, maybe seven feet away from her when my mother cut Harvey a lethal look, her grip on my hand loosening as she fell back. "What are you doing?" I tugged her back into my side.

My mother glanced her way, then back at me, drawing her own conclusions and needing no conversation about it. "I need a moment with my daughter," she said, looking solely in my direction.

Harvey backed up, like an animal caught in the hunter's scope, bracing for the shot. "I'm right here," she promised, giving me the courage I desperately needed.

"Really?" I turned to my mother, not angry with Harvey, but with this woman who refused to see me as someone capable of my own decisions.

"I came to talk sense into you, not to meet your girlfriend." She sneered, like this monumental point of self-discovery for me meant absolutely nothing to her.

I shook my head, unable to come to terms with her way of thinking. "She's everything I ever wanted. I just want you to meet her," I tried to reason.

"Wake up, Antônia. I want my daughter back." Her voice echoed, too deeply burrowed in my mind to ignore.

How many times had she told me to wake up? Like my dreams weren't enough to go on, my hopes and aspirations weren't enough to chase, because they weren't worth it to *her*.

"I wish you'd take a second to know me," I whispered.

"I just want my daughter." She shook her head, her words penetrating a barrier of the armor my new family had equipped me with.

I couldn't hold my anger back anymore. "You never listen!" I exploded. "You haven't been listening this entire time! You sent me back to this godforsaken town, and I fell in love here. I'm staying here!" I pulled the helmet off, sorrow tracking its way down my cheeks and rinsing the sweat from my face.

"I just want my daughter," she repeated silently, a tear falling down her cheek as we stood a foot apart.

The closest we'd gotten in nearly six years.

I didn't allow her any more proximity than a phone call. The sting of her blade was so much sharper in person, and here she was, ready to cut me down all over again, as if I was a teenager.

"Wake. Up." Her voice was sharp, no longer a request, but a demand.

"And if I tell you I'm staying here?" I asked.

"I'm not ready to say goodbye." She shook her head.

"It's not your choice, mãe." I used the endearment in our native tongue.

She reached out, grasping my hand, the feel of her warm skin sending a rush down my body.

"Harvey?" I called out into what felt like an endless abyss, panic coursing through my body and washing me with dread.

"Harvey!" I screamed, my eyelids fluttering quickly, my vision rendering useless. A nauseating dizziness taking hold, and a searing pain exploded like hot white light inside me.

With my mother's hand still there, I reached for support, but before I could fall to the ground, the world spun, and I was standing next to her again, overlooking a body in a hospital bed.

"Harvey?" My voice was a squeak now, even as I begged for her, but it wasn't Harvey who laid there.

My mother's thumb rubbed soft circles against the top of my pale, lifeless hand.

"What the f-"

"Wake. Up," my mother breathed, barely a whisper this time.

I choked on shallow bursts of air that couldn't fill my lungs, until I shook, screaming for help to whoever might answer. But there was only one person I wanted, one person I needed.

"Harvey." My rasped shout tore through my throat one final time before defeat conquered.

"Her brain activity is decreasing every day. Even if she was to wake up, she would likely never talk, walk, or move."

The man in the white coat barely looked up from the clipboard as he delivered the news.

"You're asking me to give up on my daughter." My mother's words were a dagger through my chest.

She'd said something similar before, recently, on the phone.

"I'm telling you to consider the life she would live, even in the *best* case scenario here, Dr. Da Silva." He was dry, typical of someone numb to this kind of pain.

"I need a moment alone with her, please." Her eyes stayed on my body laying in that hospital bed, never turning to give the doctor her full attention, even as he walked out of the room to grant her the privacy she'd requested.

"If you could see me now, Tônia." My mother chuckled under her breath, the tears falling freely down her face.

I couldn't cry. I couldn't feel much; I could only see. I could only spectate. I placed my hand on her shoulder, and her head turned briefly in my direction before she turned back to the body on the bed.

"You'd probably be throwing a fit right now, telling me you have too much unresolved business to die." She cupped her mouth, a mixture of a sob and a laugh leaving her while she shook.

Grief was a strange thing.

We had the most complicated relationship, one that deserved the most critical analysis by a studied professional, and yet we thrived off our toxic symbiosis.

My mother, my enemy, my best friend.

I couldn't live a day without her. Now, she would have to bury me, her only child, her most dreaded failure, the only accomplishment she never claimed.

A sense of calm washed over me like a nurturing embrace.

My frail body withered into nothing on that very bed, in front of my eyes. My mother remained, mourning the inevitable reality she'd soon be facing.

She was terrible at funerals—too much attention on those grieving and not on the dead for her taste.

Standing up from the edge of the hospital bed, she wiped her hand on her skirt before lifting her chin. She stared at me like she could actually see me as I was, standing there in front of her. The bed disappeared behind her, and soon, the entirety of the room was gone, faded into nothing but white, black, and everything in between.

I couldn't discern colors. I couldn't tell if it was too bright or too dark, if I was feeling hot or cold, or if I was even drawing air into my lungs. I was everything and nothing all at once.

"You understand what is happening?" she asked, her voice sounding like my mother's and yet a mixture of every voice I'd ever heard in my life. It was disorienting, hard to focus.

"I'm dead," I breathed.

A microscopic movement of her head assured what I could already feel magnanimously obvious inside me.

"When did it happen?" I asked, already knowing the answer.

"When you crashed into the tree," the deity-like voice answered.

Had I been able to feel panic, it would have wrapped itself around me. Instead, the words came out freely, no labor on their part. "Everything that happened, Harvey, it—"

"Was part of your process," the voice explained.

A lifetime of grief submerged me, pulling me under, drowning me, filling every crevice and crack in my soul, expanding until there was nothing left to feel.

"Now what?" My voice felt hollow, devoid of anything real.

"Now you cross over. You go do what it is souls do when their time in their fleshy confines have come to an end," she explained.

"I can't stay here?" Maybe this was heaven, and if it was, I would have made any trade off, sold my soul to any Devil who could guarantee me an eternity with Harvey.

"In a made-up relationship your brain decided to create as it shot off its final sparks of consciousness through its dying neurons in an attempt to process the last bit of things you felt you needed to work through and experience before death? No, you cannot stay here." It almost sounded like laughter and song combined coming from her mouth.

"But I loved her." A hole emerged in the center of my chest.

"Maybe you'll love again, in some other time, some other life, maybe more sure of yourself from the beginning." It almost sounded like a promise, one too good to be true.

"This isn't fair. I don't want to leave." I shook my head, refusing to accept the truth, unable to feel anger yet drowning in it.

"Whoever said life was fair never met death, sweet child." She finally named herself, her bony fingers caressing the edge of my face. "Are you ready?" Her voice called to me like silver bells chiming in the wind.

"What if, at the end, it just starts all over?" I asked, looking up at her with hope. The image of my mother was now gone, and the bony figure draped in a beautiful, black velvet robe tilted its skull at me as if in thought.

Out of her mouth came a song of sorrow. "I wouldn't know."

"You don't know what's on the other side?" I approached, no longer afraid.

"I cannot die, so I cannot know. It is a gift only you possess, of which I am eternally envious." Her bony hand extended to me.

I snorted in amusement, unable to believe that Death could be envious of us, as if the end was just as important as what happened in the middle. Whatever was waiting for me began to draw me like a magnet, a pull I could no longer fight, one I'd been feeling since the minute I hit my head but ignored.

The scariest part about death was not knowing what happened to the people we left behind. Yet here I was, fully sure that everything would be okay. My mother would mourn, her heart would break, but she would heal, and she would go on, head down into her work until she no longer felt the pain of my loss.

My father would cry, an occurrence so rare, it could be counted on a single hand.

A few friends would show up, but none would tell stories of me. They would simply pay their respects and say how unfair it was.

But Death was right.

Fairness had nothing to do with this. We lived and we died.

And my time had come.

A gift only we possess.

"Well then." I looked back at her. "I guess I better not waste this gift. One thing about me, bony lady—I'm not one to back down from a challenge." I smirked, dropping down to one knee to tighten the laces on my quads.

The track stretched out below me, nothing but light as far as I could see, the skeleton now gone, the only thing ahead a straight shot to the light. A cascade of rainbow stretched out beneath my feet, a path toward the unknown.

I took a deep breath, closing my eyes and letting a smile curve its way through my lips.

Here goes nothing.

PORTUGUESE WORDS
(NOT NECESSARY FOR ENJOYMENT OF STORY; MOST WORDS ARE TRANSLATED WITHIN THE TEXT)

Beijos - kisses

Cruz Credo - Holy cross / interjection - used as "holy shit" or "heaven forbid."

Cheirinho - a little sniff, a Brazilian way of greeting a loved one depending on region.

Eu não sei por que eu perco meu tempo com você. Tu não cresce - I don't know why I waste my time on you. You don't grow up.

Feijoada - A black bean dish that is slow cooked with various pork meats.

Ossinho de Sabiá - Bird-boned.

Oi – hi.

Pobrezinhos - poor things.

Porra – literal translation: jizz, used as an interjection "fuck/shit/damnit."

Que tragedia - what a tragedy.

Respeito – respect.

Tchau – bye.

ACKNOWLEDGMENTS

My incredible team of Alpha, Betas and sensitivity readers. This truly was a labor of love, and this story passed through so many hands to make sure it would be told in the best way possible. Thank you all for your dedication to my skaters, and the broken parts of me. I'm endlessly in your debt.

To the gayest team of editors to ever exist, this was the most fun I've ever had allowing people into my brain.

Brianna, my muse, my sounding board, my everything. These characters don't come to life until you've touched them. Thank you for loving my girls and thank you for the most beautiful cover in the world.

Naomi, you live rent free inside my soul, I don't know that I can write a book without you anymore, thank you for tolerating my existence.

Amy, I love you. Thank you for holding my hand through this life.

R.N Barbosa, for the developmental edits, for making me feel like this book had purpose. For making my words matter.

Alexa for all of the everything that went into polishing the insanity that happens in my brain. My editor, my friend, my ARMOR. I love you.

Angela, Erica, Chris, Christina S, Dakota, Christina C,

Jenn, Louise, Alex, Nelka, Nika, Jessie K, and Jessie A, Shaye, - Thank you, to the moon and back for everything.

Hailey S., you make the good sparks in my brain go off and I'm grateful for your light.

The council, for all the counseling. Y'all know. Nemmy, Chalan, Elle, Smash, Leo I adore you, thank you for holding me up while I wrote this.

Zazu, for always reaffirming me that my autistic experience is valid. Rowan, for reaffirming that my queer identity is valid. Ruthie for reaffirming that my mixed race identity is valid.

Margaret, for holding my hand and my leash. Thank you for keeping me together.

The real life Cat, who is nothing like our heroine, but has all the love my heart could ever withstand. Thank you for growing up beside me, thank you for being my soul-person.

My amazing ARC team.

My infinites, for decades of love now.

The many people who cheer me on regardless of my faults, Haven, Katie S, Tiara, Lori, Brooke, Eunice, Alyssa P, Jennifer R, Jennifer C, Susan C, Mila, Meghan, and if I missed anyone I'll just ruminate about it for the rest of my life.

The groups and queens that run them that I would be absolutely no one without like: Sam S and the Booktok Baddies, Shannon C and Spicy Booktok, Dark & Disturbed (Danielle & Katelin), I have so much love and appreciation for all of you.

Chelsea C., for everything you've ever done for me, and for being a friend and a cheerleader.

Hawk. For fucking Hawking into my life and now I have to build a birdcage to keep you in because I'll never let you go.

Marie Maravilla, for encouraging me to stick with this ending because it was the most Santana ending to ever exist.

Clicia, prima, amiga, te amo. Thank you for teaching me what it means to be yourself with pride.

My Lonnies, there were many of you, and I wouldn't have made it without you.

My husband, thank you for loving all the parts of me.

Dani, my incredible agent and everyone at SBR.

Kris - The real Devil's Dame, thank you for letting me use your name for our roller derby league.

Hank-Her-Knickers-Off for carrying me out of that track like a real-life version of the movie *The Bodyguard* when my leg turned into a noodle.

Brawly-Pop for forcing me to my first practice, and to every G-D*mn member of the C.A.R.D league who made me feel like family during my time on eight wheels.

I haven't been the same since.

My mother, my best friend, thank you for never giving up on me.

And to every girl who ran marathons in my mind. I wrote this for you.

ABOUT THE AUTHOR

Santana Knox is the pen name of a Brazilian author living in the United States.

Santana got tired of letting the voices in their head drive them crazy, and decided to write down the stories they were begging to tell instead. A lover of the unusual and a hopeless romantic when it comes to toxic villains, Santana's books should always be taken with a grain of salt, specifically the kind that keeps demons away.

To enter her cult, join her Facebook reading group: Santana Knox's Heathens

ALSO BY SANTANA KNOX

NEXT:

False Start - Book 2

Shredded Hearts Duet

DARK-ROMANCE:

Heartless Heathens -

A stand alone, why-choose, gothic-romance.

The Reina Del Cártel Trilogy:

Queen Of Nothing - Book 1

Reign Of Ruin - Book 2

Empire Of Carnage - Book 3

Diablos Locos Motorcycle Club:

No Place For Devils - Book 1 (Stand alone)

NOVELLAS:

No Way Out - An Erotic Horror

Dreams Of Truth - A Dark Romantasy